Last One Out
Shut Off the Lights

Last One Out Shut Off the Lights

Stories

Stephanie Soileau

Little, Brown and Company

New York Boston London

Little, Brown and Company
Hachette Book Group
1290 Avenue of the Americas, New York, NY 10104
littlebrown.com

First Edition: July 2020

Little, Brown and Company is a division of Hachette Book Group, Inc. The Little, Brown name and logo are trademarks of Hachette Book Group, Inc.

The publisher is not responsible for websites (or their content) that are not owned by the publisher.

The Hachette Speakers Bureau provides a wide range of authors for speaking events. To find out more, go to hachettespeakersbureau.com or call (866) 376-6591.

Copyright acknowledgments appear on page 241.

ISBN 978-0-316-42340-3
LCCN 20220932868

10 9 8 7 6 5 4 3 2 1

LSC-C

Printed in the United States of America

for Maude and Herman and Byron—
I'll see y'all after while.

Contents

Contents

He asked me would you jump into the water with me
I told him no way baby that's your own death you see

—Lucinda Williams, "2 Kool 2 Be 4gotten"

Last One Out
Shut Off the Lights

So This Is Permanence

For the first time since she gave birth, Sarah was left alone with her new baby. Her mother and sister—run ragged for two weeks seeing to duties that Sarah avoided by, say, hanging out in sitz baths for hours with a vampire novel— had escaped at last, back to work, back to high school. Ever since the later months of her pregnancy, after she had packed up the contents of her locker, turned in her textbooks, and left high school, apparently for good, Sarah had taken to her room, giving herself over completely to sleepless hours alone with the growing boulder of a belly and the strangely com- forting idea that if only she were a spider, she might cast this thing off on a windowsill in a bundle of silk and let it hatch on its own. Her attitude after the birth was no better. But Sarah had promised herself and her mother that she would rally, and to her credit, she had successfully fed and changed the baby twice the afternoon before.

On Monday morning she heard none of her mother and sister's bustle to tend the baby and get themselves ready for work and school, nor did she wake when her sister, on the way out, quietly opened the bedroom door and wheeled in the Pack 'n Play. Of course, they both fully expected Sarah to loaf in bed until the crying reached decibels impossible to ignore. But she did not. Only moments after her mother backed the car out of the driveway her alarm went off, for last night, in a sleepless agitation, Sarah had been inspired.

From her closet she extracted four wire hangers, and she took a roll of twine from a shelf in the laundry room. After some digging, she found pliers in her father's neglected tool chest, which had once been so impeccably organized but now, not even a year after his death, wouldn't close because of the odd angles at which the women tossed in the hammer, level, screwdrivers, and wrenches. Having laid the hangers, twine, and pliers on the kitchen table, Sarah took a peek at the Pack 'n Play. The baby was starting to stir. This was fine. She was expecting this. She knew exactly what to do.

In the hospital, the nurses had tried to teach her how to slip an arm under the baby's bottom and up toward his head, how to grip the head gently but firmly, like an egg. At the time, she simply refused to learn, and this caused a stir among the nurses, who would wheel the baby in on a cart every three hours and fuss loudly enough for the *good* mothers up and down the hall to hear: *Whose baby is this, young lady?*

Now she scooped the baby up more or less as she had been taught, and clutched him awkwardly to her chest. Tightness spread through her breasts, this gravitational pull of milk to baby, baby to milk. She felt a fleeting impulse—like the one that compelled her sometimes at the grocery store to pocket a blossom-pink lipstick or a sequined headband—to lift her shirt over her breast and press her nipple to the baby's mouth. It was mortifying and exhilarating, this feeling, and she would just as soon forget it.

Sarah clutched the baby tighter and poked a bottle of formula at his mouth. She whispered his name, which her mother had given because Sarah had not bothered to think of one, and leaned close to his head, smelling powder and a lingering stink from the diaper, and underneath all that, something almost nice, like her own hair when she had not washed it, or the foreign-familiar scent of another person that hid under perfume.

When he was done after only two ounces, she propped him up in his carrier, stationed him too on the kitchen table, and left the rest of the formula on the counter for later.

If Sarah had once been curious, it was so long ago that she hardly remembered what it felt like, or what she might have been curious about. The anoles in the camellia bushes? Penguins? She still loved music—that was a constant—but only in the way most teenage girls loved music, that is to say, enough to mold a flimsy identity from it, but not enough to pick up a guitar and search for chords or scratch lyrics on napkins at cafés. Certainly not enough—or in the right way—to beg her mother for lessons and her own instrument. Even if her parents would have paid for lessons. Which they wouldn't have.

But where had everything else gone? To the top shelves and buried corners of closets, then to garage sales. Now recovered and laid out on the kitchen table, the remaining artifacts of Sarah's dead interests were these: a shark's jaw from a field trip to Galveston Island, a five-inch plastic penguin, a shoebox of rubber Smurfs. As a supplement to these things, Sarah brought out a stack of raggedy *National Geographics*.

The baby, she realized, could be her coconspirator. In the empty house, she could finally show herself, not only to herself but to this other creature.

She held the penguin close to the baby's eyes and wiggled it. "Emperor penguins are the largest of all the penguins," she said. "And what's cool is the lady penguins lay the eggs and then go off to sea and forget about them, but the daddy penguins stay and carry the eggs on top of their feet. You'd be in a heap of trouble if I was a penguin. Ha ha."

She knotted a little noose of twine and slipped it around the penguin's neck.

"And sharks!" she said, picking up the gaping skeletal jaw. "One day you'll love sharks. One day, when you get a little older, we'll watch *Jaws*."

With no one to see and conclude that whatever she was feeling was not the right thing, or worse, that it *was* the right thing and she would be a good little mother after all, Sarah—she couldn't help herself—kissed her baby on his smooth, round forehead and let him curl his hand around her finger. They held on to each other like that for a little while, and she thought that at last they had reached an understanding, come to an agreement.

By noon, the mobile was well under way. Sarah had manipulated the wire hangers until, all joined together, they formed an asterisk that could be hung from its center. She dangled the penguin from one arm of the asterisk, the shark jaw from the next. These she counterbalanced with a constellation of Smurfs carefully arranged on the opposite arms.

Still, there were gaps to fill. She turned to the old *National Geographics*. Most of the best pictures had already been plundered for school projects, but Sarah found that her aesthetics had changed. Whereas she once might have cut out the prettiest—seals, tigers—or else the most revolting—insects, innards—she now lingered on humans, masked dancers, totems, and statues, on faces reconstructed from prehistoric skulls and given intelligent, watchful eyes under their apish brows. She cut out the skulls and the faces, and the in-between stages of their restoration, and pasted them to pieces of the shoebox. As they dried, she attached these too to the arms of the mobile.

The baby had fallen asleep, and all around his carrier on the kitchen table and scattered across the floor were bits of paper and twine, small puddles of glue, and sharp little bits of metal that had snapped off the hangers. The mobile itself lay in a tangle in the middle of the mess. Sarah felt a little too focused, and a little gnawed; she was both the pencil and the teeth that chewed it. It would be good to have a cigarette, but there were none in the house, and she was just deciding that the baby would probably sleep through a ten-minute trip to the convenience store on the corner when she heard her mother's car outside.

As soon as Sarah's mother opened the door, her expectant smile—*Where's that baby? There's that precious baby!*—turned to horror. "What on earth?" she said.

Sarah wiped at the spilled glue with a ball of torn magazine pages. The baby opened his eyes and wiggled.

"Sarah, you left this out?" Her mother snatched the bottle of formula from the counter, de-nippled it and dumped the contents into the sink. "Sometimes I think you've got no sense. Did you remember to boil the water first?" She sniffed the empty bottle. "And this mess, you're going to clean this up before you do anything else." With her giant sack of a purse still on her shoulder, Sarah's mother shook out a new trash bag and swiped scraps into it. "For goodness' sake, Sarah. I can't do it all."

"Stop! I was making something," Sarah said.

But there was no stopping her mother. Sarah's projects—and there had been few—had always upset the equilibrium of their house, had always been a dreadful, galling inconvenience. Since Sarah's father had died, her mother had been forced to get a job—her first and only job, ever—in the records department of the hospital, and her will to dominate the household had grown as a result, her home and daughters becoming more and more like unruly colonies in an overextended empire.

"Come on," Sarah said to the baby. He was huffing and tossing his arms around, gearing up for a cry. Sarah gathered up the mobile and the baby carrier, and left her mother holding the trash bag.

In her bedroom, she hung the mobile from a blade of the ceiling fan and tried to distract the baby with it. The baby's eyes opened and rolled, dizzy in his floppy head. He could not focus on anything for more than an instant of stupid amazement. Sarah realized with frustration that this was probably for the best. If she were one week old and had to look at that hideous spidery contraption hanging over her head at night, she'd—well, she'd scream, or puke, or piss her sheets. Maybe all three. Now, what kind of mother would inflict such a thing on her child?

Beneath Sarah's bedroom window was a row of thick camellia bushes that she'd never believed she could jump into or over without hurting herself. They were a great deterrent, these bushes, and Sarah, in most things, was easily deterred. But on Friday night she decided she would do it. For the first time in her life, she would catapult herself over the camellia bushes—courage, courage—not for long, only to walk down to the convenience store for smokes: ten, fifteen minutes tops, because for Christ's sake she just needed some air.

She had improvised maternity wear out of her death metal T-shirts, ripping them up the front and stringing chains of safety pins across the gap, then adding more pins as the months passed. It wasn't a bad look, she thought. She took away some of the pins and put on one of these shirts, along with a gauzy black skirt and boots; her cozy old ripped-up jeans still wouldn't close around her belly. After her sister had gone out and her mother to bed, Sarah brought the baby with her into the bathroom and spent an hour drawing cat's-eye points of eyeliner nearly to her temples, blackening her lips, and teasing her indigo hair into a masterpiece of abstract impressionism, a blown-forward asymmetrical arch that plunged down into a jagged fringe over her right eye. She inspected herself in the mirror and found she looked like hell, in the best possible way.

What would her poor old father have thought? In the old days, he would have shaken his head, lit up another cigarette, and gone back to watching the TV. He might have said, as he had when she first experimented with eyeliner and lipstick, *Has your mother seen that stuff on your face?* And if it came down to it, if her mother made too much fuss, he might have done his fatherly duty and succumbed to the idea of a spanking, threatening Sarah without much conviction, as he had done once or twice over smaller transgressions. But she didn't dress like that then. In the weeks before he died, when Sarah first turned up at the hospital looking like an imploded star, her father only winked at her as though they were sharing a joke and groaned for more Dilaudid. While her father was sick, sneaking out was never necessary; dressed any which way she wanted, she would simply exit by the front door, her mother too exhausted, too sad and distracted to do anything about it.

Back in her bedroom, Sarah put on some quiet music and painted her fingernails until the baby finally fell asleep. Just in case he should start to cry, she built a soft nest of blankets and pillows on the floor of the closet and nestled him into it.

Only ten or fifteen minutes, definitely no more than twenty.

She turned out the closet light and quietly closed the door.

She perched on the windowsill for a while, gauging the distance to the ground. Finally, Sarah gathered her skirt, launched herself over the tops of the bushes, and tumbled to the grass, bones atingle from the impact, as suddenly and bewilderingly free as a cat fallen from a balcony.

★ ★ ★

She heard the kids in the parking lot before she saw them, their loud country music and a girl yelling, "Hey, heeeyyy. Get off me!" A group of about a dozen were clustered on the bed, the roof, and the hood of someone's pickup truck, like crows on a dead rhinoceros. Sarah scanned the group for her sister, and when she was sure her sister was not among them, she revealed herself in the buzzing orange light of the parking lot.

Normally she would have ducked under her hair and slid quickly past these kids. She knew them from school. She didn't hate them, they didn't hate her, but they didn't know quite what to do with each other. After all, what could Sarah find to say to girls who went to church on Wednesday nights and then again on Sundays, who gathered every few months in front of the Walmart to testify and wash cars for Jesus? Mostly, though, she resented the way that, when pressed to be cordial, the perkier ones always tried dutifully yet warily to draw her out.

But tonight she was high on her daring. She felt a reckless urge to wander a frontier, hop a whaling ship. Short of that, she'd settle for climbing to the top of that truck and having a cigarette or two before she went home. So after she bought herself a pack of smokes, she lit up and squinted at the group of kids to find one she could casually flag down. There was among them one boy, Brent Stelly, who was sort of a floater. He was as likely to tuck in his shirt for a Wednesday-night church service with the Baptists—his family was French-Catholic, like Sarah's—as to deck himself out all in black, plunge a safety pin through his earlobe, and spend the night wandering back roads with Sarah's strange tribe.

"Sarah girl!" He leapt off the hood of the truck and jogged up to her, holding out his fist, wide silver rings on every finger. "*Comment ça va*, my cher-ree?" Seventeen years old and small, bouncy, Brent Stelly aimed to be everyone's favorite uncle from the boondocks. He was the youngest son of a huge family of Cajun fishermen-turned-roughnecks, and he played it up, the wild Cajun, the swamp rat. His tongue rode its backwoods inflections like a bucking bull.

"*Ça va, ça va,*" Sarah said, blowing a stream of smoke. She smacked his fist with her own.

"Shoo," he said and reached for the uppermost spikes of her hair. "Can I touch?"

"Yeah, sure."

"You out for the night?"

"I guess I'm out for a little while."

Two of the girls slipped off the truck and strolled over to meet them. "Hey," said one, languidly.

The friend went in for a hug that Sarah accepted stiffly and broke quickly. "How's that new baby, sweetie?"

Sweetie.

"Um, okay, I think. I don't know. Fine? He doesn't really confide in me these days." Sarah felt the examining eyes of the girls prodding at her stomach, felt them lifting and dropping each tight, over-large breast. Or maybe, after all, they were only checking out her badass safety-pin chain mail.

"Are you coming back to school?"

"I don't know."

"What are you gonna do if you don't come back?"

"I really don't know."

"So, what's the bee-bee's name?"

"I don't know."

"Quit pulling my leg."

"I'm not pulling any legs."

"Come on, Sarah, what did you name him?"

"I didn't name him."

"Well, he's got a name, doesn't he? What is it?"

The quieter one said, "I like your shirt."

Stelly linked his arm through Sarah's, pulling her toward the truck; some kids squeezed together to make room for the two of them on the hood. They smoked and watched cars pass on the strip, then pass again, and sooner or later turn into the convenience store and pull up alongside, honk, hoot, then return to the strip for a few more laps. When Stelly slid a flask of whiskey her way, without thinking overmuch about it, Sarah drank.

Fifteen or twenty minutes turned into almost an hour, and though a distant anxiety crackled in Sarah's bones, she stayed, free from her mother's say-so and the tyranny of infant. She listened to the kids bitch and laugh about the desolate crappiness of this place, none of them, not even Sarah, realizing of course that no matter what, no matter where, adolescent years were spent cruising a strip of one kind or another; that this nervous, dreamy pacing in the dark corridors of town, this poking around for surprises in dusty corners and sounding of walls for secret passages would come to nothing much, and ultimately a good many of them would relish the onset of complacency, would become dentists and dental assistants, or flunk out of dental school and become offshore roustabouts, real-estate assessors, and school-board clerks, would buy a large house on the lakefront or a small house in a neighborhood of elderly people, marry, go to church, have babies, baptize their babies, and many other common, decent things that now, in their restiveness, most of them, especially Sarah, would call *giving in*.

Sarah and Stelly reclined next to each other against the windshield. They smoked steadily and drank when the whiskey came around. One of the boys reached inside the truck and turned the radio up for an old country song they'd all heard since kindergarten, a slow and faraway goodbye song. *On a hidden beach under a golden sun she spread a blanket that we laid down on and loved the world away.* The kids passed the flask and sang and swayed arm in arm to the lovely, aching promise of nostalgia.

It was all very bizarre, and seemed more bizarre by the minute, that Sarah should find herself in the parking lot among these kids, especially when she ought to be home—and how very, very strange that she ought to be home doing the things she ought to be home doing. Her head drooped between her knees and she remembered the startled eyes of the creature that had been extracted from her numbed lower half barely two weeks ago. It made her giggle, the thought of herself in labor, the absurd lump of her belly, the rock-star paroxysms of her face, and the blessed disembodiment as painkiller after painkiller was pumped into her. It was a joy, sure, a relief to be at last free of the weight and movement inside her. Then that creature—and here she giggled harder—that strange, groping alien they laid on her chest and insisted was hers!

When Stelly leaned into her ear now and said, "How

14

come you ain't dancing, Sarah girl?" she could hardly stand it. She quaked with laughter in spite of herself, whiskey-warm and wild, until the talking around her, the boys' teasing and the girls' shouts, stopped altogether, and she felt Stelly's arm snake around her shoulders and squeeze, then the welcome suffocation against his hard little chest, smelling first of cologne and then of human sweetness and heat.

One of the girls said, "Is she okay?"

A boy said, "I think she's laughing."

"Is she laughing?"

A hand touched Sarah's back. "Are you okay, sweetie?"

"She's okay," Stelly said. Then he whispered to Sarah, "Let me take you home, *chère*. It's time you went home."

Sarah said to her knees, "Good God, I don't want to go home. Take me somewhere else."

They drove south. Each time they paused at a crossroads, Stelly asked, "Which way?" and Sarah answered, "Straight. Just drive." After an hour or so, the flat, grassy pastures turned to marshes and canals, and they crossed one drawbridge after another until they finally reached the Gulf of Mexico.

The dilapidated beach resort at this time of year was nearly empty and, except for a few small and widely spaced street lamps and lighted windows, entirely dark. Sarah and Stelly left their car on the road and their shoes under the porch of a deserted camp. The water was still warm and remarkably serene, the waves low, reticent; shouting and laughing, the two bared their legs and plunged in. They made more noise than the sea itself, and this seemed to Sarah a magnificent thing.

After a while, drenched to the hips, Stelly turned back toward shore. Sarah's skirt was hiked up to her waist, waves splashed against her thighs. She tested each step with her toes and went on. A rig flickered in the far distance, so small, so isolated, that it might have been sparked by a fisherman's Zippo. It would be easy, really, to keep wading toward that light.

"Don't go too far," Stelly shouted. "Hey!"

Miles from this beach, somewhere in the middle of that moving darkness, were men and women who lived their lives like Sarah's father had, intermittently, two weeks on, two weeks off, napping on the couch or puttering in the house, yard, town for fourteen-day stretches, and just when the harder questions of living begged for answers, they were off again to the rigs, questions forgotten, decisions unmade. They were whisked away in helicopters to a place for which Sarah had no reference in her imagination. Not a trace there of family life, of children, no pictures or toys, no sentimental accumulations, the Gulf beneath and miles all around, reflecting only the rig, the night sky, and nothing of home.

"Sarah!"

"All right!" Any moment she could plunge into deeper water. "I'm coming back."

Sarah and Stelly lay down in the sand, shoulder to shoulder, wrist to wrist, foot to foot, and shared their last cigarette, brushing fingers when they passed the butt back and forth, and lingering upon casual touches just past the point of necessity. This was the sign. It could be taken or left.

For the longest time, they just lay there and breathed.

At last Stelly said, "I seen Daniel the other day at that diner off the highway."

"Yeah, he's always there."

"How come you don't tell him—you know?"

Sarah put out the cigarette, stood and brushed the sand from her skirt and hair, which had wilted in the moist air and was clinging, sticky and limp, to her forehead and neck. "Hey," she said, "want to hear my death rattle? I've been practicing, listen." She let her head sag to her chest, and a ghastly, dry croak escaped her throat. "Ghhhhaaaaaah."

"If the baby was mine," Stelly said, "I'd want to know."

She made the croaking sound again.

"Sarah."

"I'm sure he can figure it out."

"If it was mine, I'd want to do something about it." Stelly reached for her foot and traced the tendons down to her toes and to her toenails, with their half-moons of chipped black polish. From his knees he tugged at her skirt, drew her down to him, and she was on her knees too then. She heard a rush in her ears, felt a pounding of waves on her chest when their noses touched. Stelly slipped a hand under her shirt, but Sarah grabbed that hand and held it; not so long ago, her breasts had answered even the slightest touch with a humiliating trickle of warmth. She buried her face in the soft nook behind his ear. She said, "Yeah? What would you do about it?"

"I'd—" He dug his fingers into her flaccid stomach. They crept under the waistband of her skirt as he kissed her neck, her ear, her mouth, as his other hand found its way again into her shirt, groped, caressed, and stopped. "Wait," he said. He sat back on his heels. "Hold on. No."

"God," she breathed. She seized a handful of sand and threw it hard into the wind. She threw another, then another, and the fallout blew back into their faces.

"Quit it," Stelly said.

Sarah did not quit it. Stelly turned away, shielding his eyes with his arm. "Stop!"

Sarah did not stop.

"I'm taking you home."

"Fine! Take me home." She launched the next handful at his back.

He stood and dusted himself off. "Well, get dressed. Come on, get up."

She straightened her clothes, but didn't move. A gull dipped and circled just above them, trilled quietly, and then glided out over the water, where the first few fishing boats were leaving the channel and chugging toward the horizon.

"Get up, Sarah."

"No!"

"Come on, girl."

"Wait!" She clutched at his damp, sand-caked jeans. "Let's stay here. Let's live here!" Stelly shook his leg free and took her hand to pull her up, but she went limp like she would as a little girl when her mother tried to carry her to the bathtub or to church. The dead weight of her body dangled from her upstretched arm, which Stelly held firmly by the wrist. He dragged her a little way through the sand before finally giving up and letting go. Sarah let her head and arm fall at deliberately bizarre angles. "Ghhhhaaaah," she groaned.

"Come on, what are you doing?" Stelly poked her once with the toe of his boot. "Girl, get up. We have to go."

★ ★ ★

Of all the possible moods Sarah imagined she would walk into at home—resigned annoyance in the best case, wild fury in the worst—none approached the silence with which her sister met her at the door and shadowed her through the kitchen and into the living room, where the baby, rescued from the closet, now squirmed on the floor amid the debris of her sister's all-night vigil. He seemed carelessly discarded there, along with the empty soda cans and bag of potato chips, the fashion magazines and catalogs, like he might easily be swept up and tossed away. His hands flew up and wriggled in the air; according to the maternity-ward nurses, this ancient and adorable reflex meant the baby thought he was falling from the tree. *So fall,* Sarah thought and felt remorse, almost immediately.

Their mother slept on the couch with a Bible tented on her chest. In moments of distress, their mother would take up the Bible as though it were a Magic 8-Ball; asking silent questions, worrying silent worries, she would let it fall open in her lap and start reading at the first word her eyes latched on to, and always she found the kind of contorted and ambiguous relevance—or so it appeared to Sarah—that her sister found in, say, the horoscopes of *Vogue* and *Cosmo*.

Exhausted, her shoes and clothes and hair prickly with sand, Sarah went immediately, casually, to her bedroom. She rooted through disorganized, overstuffed drawers for her pajamas while her sister stood in the doorway, watching her. Finally, when Sarah flopped heavily onto her bed and heaved a most defiant sigh, her sister said, very quietly, and with more wonder than reproach, "You didn't even pick him up. You didn't even bother."

In the weeks that followed, the less effort Sarah put into the care of her baby, the less her mother and sister helped her. He might cry or be hungry or sit in his own filth much longer, but neither of them would lift a finger. Some conspiracy was afoot between them. While before her father's death there had been predictable and equal alignments in their domestic loyalties—sometimes Sarah and her sister against their mother and father; sometimes Sarah and her father against her sister and her mother—Sarah now found herself without an ally, her privacy infiltrated by this sensitive little infant spy who would blow the whistle, loudly, on any negligence or indiscretion.

Except to roll the stroller up and down the block or to run to the grocery store, with baby in tow, for formula and diapers, Sarah never left the house. She was bored. She was lonely. Not long ago, dropping out of school had seemed like the one good thing to come of all this, but now she sometimes talked about going back, and when she did, it was as though she had made an insipid comment about a character on TV, and she might get an inattentive answer but more likely she would be ignored altogether.

One Saturday around noon the baby started crying and, like an angry god, would not be appeased. Sarah cycled through every possible desire; she offered feeding, diaper-changing, entertainment, then feeding again. She sang to him from her repertoire of disturbing dirges by The Cure, Joy Division, Bauhaus, and was even getting sort of into it, inventing a two-part harmony—as nearly as one voice can—for "Love

Will Tear Us Apart" when her sister said, "Do you know how off-key you are? If you don't cut it out, *I'm* going to cry." Her mother suggested walking around with him, keeping him moving, so Sarah propped the baby on her shoulder and wandered through the house, jiggling him and humming *uhhuhhuhhuhhum* in breathy bursts, a completely unmusical but comforting sound her mother used to make when she or her sister was inconsolable.

Still he cried. He cried through the afternoon and into the evening. He screamed until he was hoarse, until his whole body hiccupped, choking itself on some mysterious distress. He clawed at blankets, at Sarah, at himself until he drew blood on his own neck and she had to mitten his hands in tiny socks: a tiny straitjacket for a tiny madman.

This was not part of their agreement. This bawling thing—this was the very creature that had moved unbearably in her body for months, yet he did not know Sarah from anyone else, and in fact he did not seem to know person from thing. When he scratched himself, he did not know the cause of the pain or how to stop it—he could not even tell himself from himself. How could she love a creature like this? How did people find it in themselves to love such a thing?

Sarah knew that this was the point when some mothers lost it completely, when Dumpsters and rivers started to look like good alternatives. And Sarah did not know herself well enough to be certain where she actually meant to go when she snatched her mother's keys off the kitchen counter and announced that she was taking the baby for a ride to see if maybe, by the grace of God, that would shut him up.

★　★　★

Nearly a year ago, just after Christmas, Sarah had gone to the hospital and found her father—who had been articulating the most precise and vivid hallucinations only the day before—entirely receded, the skin of his hand and cheek a dry, spongy bark, his wasted body too dense, too heavy to be budged by the tiny kernel of life lodged and buzzing in his throat. Her mother and sister would wait with him until the end, but Sarah called her friends to pick her up, and until he was laid out in a casket four days later, she did not see her father again.

She spent those four days mostly with Daniel, in self-imposed exile in a freestanding backyard kitchen that Daniel Sr. had built when Mrs. Daniel banned the cooking of meats in her house. He practiced guitar there, the younger Daniel, because that had been not banned but annoyingly encouraged in the main house, and often, if he'd gotten into some trouble that his parents might detect on his person, he slept there, camped out under a card table in a sleeping bag, absorbing into his clothes and long hair a pleasing aroma of garlic and gristle that he would carry around all the next day. It made Sarah hungry, being near him.

For those four days, he let her live there with him, and every night she watched him assault the guitar before she cuddled up next to his light, fluttery body and let his hands dance over her.

They were careless, it's true, but there was comfort in their carelessness. And it had not seemed possible that a boy who looked so much like a girl that new acquaintances sometimes called him—accidentally, impulsively—Danielle could ever father anyone, could ever be complicit in her body's mean betrayal of her wishes.

It baffled her even now, as she watched him through the window of the diner. He was sitting in the booth at the rear, fooling around with a pennywhistle and ignoring a conversation that came to a halt entirely when Sarah, with her wailing baby, flung open the door. It was unclear to Sarah exactly what Daniel knew, or whether he had indeed drawn the obvious conclusion from the evidence presented to him. Regardless, confirmation of a host of rumors was now about to join him at the table, kicking its legs and screaming bloody murder. To discuss the situation would be, Sarah thought, redundant.

"Hello," she said and shoved the baby carrier into the seat between herself and a boy she knew vaguely from last spring's geometry class. Daniel dropped a curtain of hair over his face and would not be coaxed out by greeting or question. Across the table next to Daniel was a boy Sarah didn't recognize. She appropriated his ashtray and shook a pack of cigarettes that was lying on the table. For a moment the new boy made eye contact with her. "Can I bum a smoke?" she said.

He said something she couldn't hear over the crying. "What?"

"I said it's my last one."

"Do you have one, Dan?"

"Nope. Quit."

"You didn't quit," she said.

"This is just crazy," said the boy from geometry class. "I

mean, I can't even believe it, right? Can you believe this came out of Sarah?"

"You're so fucking stoned," Daniel said, and started a different tune on the pennywhistle, something twittering and ticklish that for a moment diverted the baby's attention from his own misery.

"Wow. That's the first time he's stopped crying in hours," Sarah said. "Are you all really telling me there are no cigarettes at this table?"

She got up to bum one from an old man at the counter and when she sat down again there was whispering between Daniel and the stranger. The stranger quivered with stifled laughter and Daniel grinned under his hair, his lips pulled back, teeth gripping the pennywhistle. A snicker sputtered down the pipe and seemed to flick out like a tongue.

"Where did you find that thing anyway?" she said.

"It's mine," said the stranger.

"Oh. And who are you?"

"He's our guy," said the boy from geometry.

"You're their guy?"

"Yeah."

"What the fuck does that mean?"

More whispering commenced on the other side of the table. Tucking the pennywhistle and a cigarette lighter into a back pocket, Daniel shooed their guy out of the booth and together they skulked off toward the men's room. The restroom door slapped closed behind the two boys, and that was all there was to it.

The problem was that she understood how he felt, she

really did, and she could not hold it against him. If she'd been in his position, she would have treated her the same way, no question. In fact, she would have gone further. She would have used every trick of math and misremembered chronology, all the hostile confidence of forensics and gossip, to prove what could not be proven, to make true what was so unmistakably false. And the names she would have called herself! The things she would have insinuated! And she—the *she* she actually was—the sixteen-year-old mother of a baby confronting the seventeen-year-old father of that baby—would at least have been granted the dignity of outrage, instead of this slow, creeping embarrassment, this paltry and invisible disintegration.

She would not have sat there and said nothing at all, she would not have sneaked into the men's room like a worm to get high on whatever they were getting high on.

Or else she would have. In fact, she would have, so she was back to this after all: she could not blame him.

The boy from geometry swooped down on her baby with a crazy face, going, "I'm gonna eat you! I'm gonna eat you!" The baby was twisting up his mouth and jerking his feet, sucking in air for another screech.

"Hey," Sarah said, "can you watch him for a minute? I need to get something out of my car."

She truly had not planned it, but it couldn't have been easier. Not the old man sipping coffee at the counter, or the two young roustabouts eating fried cheese, or the woman playing video poker, or the waiter who moved aside to let Sarah pass—not one of them protested or even raised their heads as she walked out the door, started the car, and simply drove away, leaving her child there in the booth, like leftovers or a purse.

This interstate, if one took certain exits and cloverleaf turn-arounds, led exactly nowhere, and while Sarah was looping around Lake Charles and Sulphur at seventy miles per hour, past the petrochemical plants along the lakeshore, past the mega-stores and chains on the outskirts of town, the seafood markets and shotgun houses of the older neighborhoods, over the bridge and back around to the petrochemical plants again, she was debating whether she, like certain of her rougher cousins, had what it took to actually drive away from this place and toward another one, effectively stealing her mother's car, sleeping on strangers' couches or in strangers' beds, working a more depressing job than she had ever feared until she was inevitably apprehended and condemned to a juvenile detention center for the rest of her adolescence. She just might.

It was so hard to do anything about anything. It was so hard to love anything, and she could not find a way to love anything more, or to hoist herself out of this pit. She saw the shadows of others moving around up there; sometimes a face peeked down. Where was the rope?

When she had first discovered she was pregnant, she searched the yellow pages for abortion clinics, of which there were, of course, none. So she called a hospital and asked evasive questions in all the wrong ways, got no answer, and fretted in her room late at night until several months had passed and her pants no longer fit and she had to tell her mother. By then, of course, it was too late to do anything about it, and even if it weren't, her mother would never have allowed it, would have rejected the idea out of hand and been appalled that it had occurred to her daughter in the first place. If Sarah were a different kind of person, she might have begged a ride into another town, worked connections, asked bold questions.

Instead she was left with this impossible choice, and no way of knowing how to make it.

She imagined the boys—and this made her laugh out loud—re-abandoning the baby on the front steps in an elaborately stealthy maneuver, a trio of gutter-punk anarchists depositing a home-cooked bomb. She could also imagine Daniel hunching over his newborn son in the back seat of a crummy and rattling old hooptie, abashed as she had been by the growing resemblance between that tiny, near-formless face and his own.

One day the child would speak to her, would ask her questions and develop preferences for, say, drums over trumpets, for cucumbers over tomatoes, would—in other words—become remarkable in the small ways that people inevitably become remarkable to those who must observe them every day. But now, what was he? He was one more thing that failed to interest her.

For a moment, when he was first handed to her in the hospital—there was something. He had been so much like a featherless, fledgling bird, but not in the way her mother or the nurses thought. *Look at those little bird lips, look at my hungry little bird.* No.

More like the sad, naked beasts she'd seen as a little girl

in the bleachers of dolphin shows and football games, fallen like ripe figs from their nests in the rafters, and crushed, or soon to be, jerking their heads on stem-like necks, jerking their not-yet wings.

She had longed to squash them under her shoe, and to cradle them in her hands. She had wanted to touch their rubbery skin, to pry open their blind, bruise-blue eyes, to hide them in a shoebox and to bake them in a pie. And whenever she reached for one, whenever her exasperated mother grabbed her collar, yanked her up onto the bleachers and knocked the filthy, dying creature from her hands, her father's complacent drawl had spread over her like an umbrella. *Let her be, she's fine. Just let the child do.*

An Attachment Theory

At the mobile-home dealership on Highway 14, a salesman in a short-sleeved button-down shirt and bow tie ushered Kay and her seven-year-old daughter, Lindsey, on a tour from unit to unit. He was gentlemanly, solicitous, patient, like an undertaker showing caskets. The day was already blazing at ten in the morning. The trailers—bared to the sun on the treeless lot, their windows and doors sealed shut, their central AC units virgin and dormant—sucked up the heat, held it, and blew it hard in their faces whenever the salesman opened a door.

"I can't open my eyes!" Lindsey cried the first time, and raised her hands as though shielding herself from the attacking beak of a bird. "Why does it smell like that?"

"They use formaldehyde in the carpet," the salesman said, apologetically. "A preservative." He waved the door to make a breeze.

Kay had saved as much as she could. She wanted a house, like a real house, with no tongue or tie-downs, but she had only enough down payment for this, a trailer—manufactured home, whatever—and it would have to do. Her older brother, Charlie, recently laid off from PPG, had given up his apartment and reclaimed his childhood bedroom, where Kay and Lindsey had been living for the last seven years. Now they were back in the other bedroom with Kay's older sister, Fleda (who worked at the school board and made barely enough for groceries), and her younger sister, Beryl (who got disability and wasn't quite right in the head). Their father stayed in the third bedroom, in a king-size bed he once shared with their relentlessly angry, blisteringly reproachful mother, whose death from cancer a dozen years ago had brought a guilty relief to the house but had freed up no further space.

The salesman showed them doublewides, 18 x 70s, 16 x 80s, 14 x 60s. Trailers with kitchens at the front, with kitchens in the middle. In every one, Kay thumped and pressed the Sheetrock walls, searching for signs of weakness, a system prescribed by her over-helpful male coworkers at Southern Pipe and Supply. *Just like picking out a watermelon. If you hear something funny with the acoustics, pass it on by.*

No matter how the walls sounded, solid or hollow, under the influence of the sympathetic salesman Kay was enticed to marvel at every departure from the most basic floor plan, those little touches that did in fact make a trailer into a home.

"Look, baby," Kay exclaimed, "built-in bookshelves! A garden tub!"

Lindsey did not want to move out. They doted on her, all the many adults in Kay's father's house. Who got Lindsey her favorite snacks at the Market Basket? Paw Paw. Who played puppy dog when Mama just wanted to watch *The X-Files* and eat potato chips? Tante Beryl. Who took Lindsey to the library, searched for Waldo, read in voices, and was always ready with the hot-glue gun? Tante Fleda. They doted so much on the child that Kay was irrelevant.

When the salesman introduced with portent the blue Champion at the end of the row—"I believe," he said, "that *particular* home has a kitchen *island*"—Kay knew she'd found exactly what she and Lindsey needed, a shore where they could wash up together, subject at last to no other law or influence.

"And this could be your room," Kay said, wrapping her hand around Lindsey's nape and coaxing her into the larger of the Champion's two bedrooms. The carpet, itself a temperate grayish-blue, was accented by sprigs of grayish-blue flowers that crawled the paneling. "Your very own room! It's your favorite color, too."

Lindsey ducked away from Kay's hand and rubbed her fume-reddened eyes. She put a finger over one nostril and blew, rattling her congestion. "Are we done shopping now? Can we go home?"

The salesman had excused himself to the kitchen. He leaned against the island, arms crossed, head tactfully bowed. Again, Kay thumped the walls, but this time like she was patting the flank of a nice little dairy cow, just won at auction. "This is home," she said. "This is going to be home."

★ ★ ★

Kay had tried to get out on her own before, sort of: with a man, Lindsey's father, of whom Lindsey had no memory, since she had never so much as seen him. Kay had met Nason at the JC Penney jewelry counter, where she had her first job out of high school. Broad-chested and gap-toothed, his fine hair cropped short, and still wearing his Olin Chemical blues, he had peered through the display glass at the birthstone rings and asked to see a simple band with a tiny inset topaz.

"That's the classiest one, if you ask my opinion," Kay said. She knew how to sell things, but she also meant it that time. "For your wife?"

"My daughter's turning ten tomorrow," Nason said. When he put out his palm, his ring finger was bare. He set the band back on the counter and held up a child's velveteen night-gown with long sleeves and lace at the throat, still on the hanger. "Can I pay for this here too?"

"What a lucky little girl," Kay said.

He asked for Kay's number. She went to write it down on his receipt, but he said, "I'll just lose that. Tell me and I'll remember." She told him and he said it back to her, half a dozen times. "I won't forget," he said. Then he got a faraway look and started reciting something that sounded like a cross between a song and a zipper going up and down. "That's Pushkin!" he said when he finished, which clarified nothing. "I have no idea what I'm saying, but boy, I've got a memory like a steel trap."

What the hell else was she doing? Polishing nose- and fingerprints off the glass display cases. Living in the same house she'd lived in all her life, with the same sisters, now grown. Why not let a nice-looking man take her for rides in his Monte Carlo? He opined on physics and poetry, which were over her head, but she sure liked to listen, the same way she'd listened to her grandparents speak French out in the country, the *ouais* and *chères* and *comment ça va*s, and to her high school English teacher quote—who was it?—John Somebody. Done. Or, no. Donne. With two *n*s.

Nason lived way out on the Calcasieu River, where he owned a house that wasn't much more than a camp, but also a bit of marsh. His daughter, by a woman he'd married briefly and divorced, was around sometimes, too. He'd buy ice cream for the daughter and Kay. Tell them to step back from the barbecue pit when the fire was too hot. Hustle them inside when lightning flashed over the river. And he hooked Kay up with a better job, doing inside sales at a pipe-and-supply warehouse where his buddy was the manager.

Kay knew Nason didn't want any more kids, but who can keep track, perfectly, of her birth control? And frankly, what birth control? When Nason asked about it, she said yes, yes. If it happened—and she didn't entirely believe it would, because what young woman does?—she thought he would take them in, her and the child. Kay would listen to him better than the last wife, show more interest, keep herself good-looking. In ten years or so, he'd be at JC Penney again, paying for another birthstone ring and a fancy nightgown.

After she settled things with the mobile-home salesman, Kay drove to the fish market on Highway 14, ordered a half dozen live catfish, most of them small enough for a seven-year-old to have caught on worms and one a little oversize, a doozy to make a story of, and asked that they be dumped, as they were, into the ice-filled cooler she'd packed into the car that morning.

So that no one else might encroach upon her house hunt, Kay had told her father, brother, and sisters that she was taking Lindsey fishing in Sweet Lake, far enough south that no one would go to the trouble of investigating. That morning she had outfitted Lindsey with sunblock and a fishing hat, then packed a lunch and two fishing poles into the car. She'd gone out to the backyard with her father's homemade worm-shocker to electrocute nightcrawlers out of the ground, tossed a dozen or so into a plastic cup with some dirt, and packed that into the car too. When her father brought out his pole and said he might as well come along, she flew into hysterics. And he couldn't really argue that after coming home every night to Lindsey already occupied with homework or her aunts or her grandfather, Kay didn't need time alone with her daughter. It was an elaborate deception but she couldn't take any chances.

"How come we can't just tell them?" Lindsey said as Kay heaved the cooler, now full, back into the trunk.

"You know how they're going to be."

In fact, even Kay didn't know how they were going to be, but it had always been her habit to hide things. First from her mother, whose fierce tongue was so easily stoked: report cards, soiled undies, boyfriends, and one small tattoo. Even after her mother died, though, Kay still hid things, whether opinions, both inflammatory and innocuous, or her pregnancy, until it couldn't be hidden anymore. Worse, she wore this weakness in the imploring sensitivity of her eyes, the willing collapse of her bones. She could tell by the way people looked at her, asked things of her, demanded them. She could tell by the fact that her daughter had no father, and worse, had no use for her mother.

In the back seat, Lindsey yanked at the shoulder strap, pulled it away from her, and let it slap back, then ducked under and sat against it. She curled one knee up to her chin. "I'll tell them if you won't," she said.

"Don't you dare."

It took three weeks for Kay to work up the nerve, three weeks of pretending at memories from the terrific fishing trip to Sweet Lake, of reciting the tale of the big one Lindsey had pulled up by herself, of hearing her father and brother recite this same tale to neighbors (Lindsey petulantly silent through all of it). Three weeks of waiting for the bank loan to come through, for a lot to open up in the park she'd chosen—a nice one with a pool, a clubhouse, regulations about awnings and skirting, not some rusted-out, hick-infested wreck like you see on the nightly news. The Southtowner Village on Nelson Road behind the Baptist church, not the Jesse James Mobile Home Park next to Hocus Pocus Liquors, a little farther down the same road.

When Kay finally fessed up, the family was gathered in the living room for dinner, Kay's sisters on the love seat, hip to hip like two plump partridges, her brother in the recliner where their mother used to sit, her father in his own always-and-forever recliner next to that one. Kay sat alone on the long sofa. TV trays bearing baking pans were propped before them. In the pans lay the cracked and emptied remains of four dozen boiled blue crabs. Watching a hurricane threaten some other coast on the Weather Channel, they had gorged themselves, snapping and cracking and slurping and sucking, splattering crab juice in a mist across their shirtfronts, and now they rested, sated, their dripping, smelly, spice- and shell-crusted hands held up and away from their bodies as if in mocking imitation of the creatures they'd consumed. Lindsey had picked at and played with her little pile of crabs for only a short time before excusing herself without a word, probably to the bathtub, where she would stew with a book until the water cooled to a point of discomfort, at which time she would dart, naked, damp and shivering, to the bedroom and slam the door behind her.

It had been a joyous feast, and the festive mood gave Kay the courage, at last, to speak up. After all her anxiety, it turned out not to be such a big damn deal. Her older sister, Fleda, always more likely to take her part than the others, said it was a good school district out there, and she would be so close to the Walmart. Her brother patted his full belly and said she could use his truck as long as she didn't expect him to lift anything.

The lone voice of dissent was her father. "*Mais,* what you going to do with *pistache*?" His pet name for Lindsey.

Her brother had not taken his eyes off the TV. Her younger sister, Beryl, scooted out the tray, rose from the love seat, collected the detritus of her meal, and carried it to the kitchen. The faucet whooshed on and pans rattled against pans. Fleda waited, watching their father, who stared down Kay with the same aghast, bereft expression he'd worn when she first told him she was pregnant. An unlit cigarette was stuck to his lower lip and drooping to his chin.

"I thought she could come here after school," Kay said. "Just until I get off work. If that's all right with you."

"Well," he said, and lit the cigarette. "If that's what you got to do." He leaned back in his recliner and turned up the volume for *Wheel of Fortune*. "Go tell her our show is on."

When Lindsey was the tiniest of babies, Kay would lock the door to keep her sisters from barging in and taking over the kissing and cooing and dandling, and she would bend her body around her daughter's body, curling a shielding arm along the baby's pink and naked back. This fragile, groping thing with rose-petal lips was *hers,* not theirs. At night or early in the morning, in the quiet of their bedroom, she was all hers. And as Lindsey learned to sit up, and then crawl, and then walk, and to say words and reach for things she wanted, Kay would have to coax her daughter away from whatever closed, locked door where she stood whimpering for her aunts or her uncle or her grandfather, pry her little fingers off the knob, carry her back to the bed, wailing sometimes. "No, baby," Kay would say, "it's time for you to be with me. *I'm* the momma."

These days, though, together in a double bed crammed between her sisters' singles, Kay and Lindsey were all elbows and knees and fights for the covers. Kay, restless and hot-natured, was always tossing blankets aside and kicking the sheets loose, so that almost nightly, Lindsey would wake in a panic and thrash her arms to free herself from the tangle of bedding. "They're all on me!" she'd whine. "I'm smothering!"

Tonight, in preparation for another battle, Lindsey was at the foot of the bed, tucking the sheets deep under the mattress, battening things down so that maybe for once they would stay put. Kay leaned against the headboard, halfway looking at a cooking magazine. The sisters were not yet in bed.

"Are you excited to have your own room, baby?"

Lindsey did a noncommittal wiggle with her shoulders and gave the sheets one last shove under the mattress. She plucked a fluffy-maned lion from the dozens of stuffed animals piled on bookshelves in the corner, hugged it to herself, and crawled under the covers. Then she curled up around the lion, her back to Kay.

"We're going to have a whole house to ourselves," Kay said. "Some peace and quiet for a change."

Lindsey did the little shoulder-wiggle again, like she was shaking off a stranger's hand, and Kay turned out the light. When Lindsey started sniffling in the dark and then shuddering and then openly weeping, Kay couldn't take it anymore. She reached her hand stealthily over to the window near the bed and tapped at the pane. Lindsey caught her breath and listened. Kay rapped the glass again, a little harder this time.

"Listen," she said. "Do you hear that?"

Lindsey's body stiffened. She clutched the sheets to her chin.

"You better quiet down," Kay said. "Or they're going to get you."

Her mobile home, all 16 x 80 feet of it, looked naked and clean next to the other homes in the row, its Sheetrock siding an unstained ashy blue, its tongue and wheels and iron knees exposed, the vinyl skirting in a bound-up pile at the back of the lot. One thin silver maple cast a little patch of shade across the driveway in the evening. She had hired the sons of her new landlord to collect in a moving van the few things in the family home that were unequivocally hers and Lindsey's: clothes and toys, the bed that the two of them had shared these seven years, the twin bed and shelves that her father had spent the last few weeks building and painting, to Lindsey's specifications, for her new room. Kay had allowed herself the indulgence of a living-room set—couch, recliner, and coffee table, obtained in a deal at Sears—and pieced together the rest of her new household's bare essentials from thrift stores and garage sales. Another indulgence was a boxful of coordinated decor from Home Interiors: prints of lopsided barns, ceramic chickens and roosters, a trio of decorative mirrors, candleholders, oil lamps, a jug of purple oil, all ordered from a catalog and delivered to her own brand-new door.

When everything had been arranged to her satisfaction, Kay went to check on her daughter's progress. Lindsey was in her room, organizing stuffed animals by species and size on a set of tall plastic shelves. Kay surveyed the exploding garbage bags, five of them, the walruses and giraffes and gorillas and German shepherds and something that Lindsey called "my beloved okapi," a weird animal that Kay had never seen in life or in pictures, with the head of a deer and zebra stripes on its haunches, a gift to her daughter from Fleda. All of these, in fact, had been given by Kay's sisters, brother, and father, except for a series of brightly colored bears in coats that Lindsey never played with or bothered to name—these Kay had given Lindsey herself.

As Lindsey straightened a slumped-over chimpanzee into a seated position on the lowest shelf, Kay sat down on the neatly made bed. She picked up the receiver of the blue princess phone on Lindsey's bedside table, just to listen to the dial tone. "I never had my *own* phone," Kay said.

Ignoring her, Lindsey busted open another bag of animals, spread its contents across the floor, and continued to sort and organize.

Kay grabbed one of the bears in coats. She removed the coat. Then she reached for the nearest animal, a rhinoceros with beady, angry eyes, and shoved its head through the coat collar, its front feet through the sleeves. She flopped the fuzz-trimmed pink hood down over its horn. "Look," she said, and made the rhino dance.

Lindsey whirled around, irritated, but then couldn't help herself and giggled. She went back to her sorting and shelving.

Kay found another clothed animal, a half-human half-cat with a rubber face and a creepy smile, done up in a lacy white dress. She stripped it nude and put the dress on a lemur.

"Stop," Lindsey said, with a quick glance over her shoulder.

Kay took the scuba gear off a teddy bear and put it on a grizzly bear, then dressed a koala in a policeman's uniform. She lined them all up on the bed.

"Stop it." Lindsey looked distressed.

"I'm helping."

"No you aren't."

"Fine," Kay said. She picked up the phone receiver again

and held it out. "Why don't you call Tante Fleda to help you, then."

Lindsey's face opened up for a second. Then, when she understood that this was not really an option, she began to undo Kay's handiwork herself.

Very early on their first Sunday morning in the new house, before Kay had changed out of her nightgown, before Lindsey had come into the kitchen to rummage for a cold breakfast in the cabinets that still smelled of pressboard adhesives, Kay's father knocked on the door, a cigarette dangling from his lips and a small, grease-sopped paper bag in hand. "Where is she?" he said.

"Still sleeping."

"Go get her. Tell her she's got donuts waiting for her."

"You didn't need to come all the way out here for that. We've got food in the house, you know."

"I know I didn't need to."

"Did you bring one for me?"

"*Mais,* no."

Kay took the bag, unrolled the top. "There are three in here."

"She always eats three. Two chocolates and a plain. That's what she likes, *mais,* that's what I brought."

Why did her own father have to be so spiteful to her? Even still, she moved aside to let him in. "Watch your ashes," she said, and cupped her hand under the precarious tip of his cigarette.

"Aw, *comme ci*! I won't let it fall," he said. He sat down in a kitchen chair, scooted away from the table, and placed the

41

bag on his knee, appraising the island. The long curl of ash promptly dropped onto his shirt and rolled down to his belly. "How come they put a cabinet in the middle of the room like that?" he said.

Before Kay could answer, Lindsey came thumping, heavy-footed, down the hall, blinking and shoving her bangs aside.

"Look what's in that bag for you," Kay's father said, and Lindsey opened the bag, took out a sticky, glistening donut, and kissed him on the cheek. Munching slowly, dreamily, she stood between his knees, leaned back against his chest. "Y'all coming to church this morning?" he asked.

"We'll go to the six o'clock mass," Kay said.

He pressed his mouth to Lindsey's ear and said in a whisper loud enough for Kay to hear, "You want to come to church with Paw Paw, *chère*?"

Kay ripped a paper towel off the roll and handed it to her daughter. "She's coming with me."

"Okay," he said.

Kay ignored him and puttered around the kitchen, doing dishes and rearranging cabinet space.

Every now and then, her father would pat Lindsey's thigh and say, *"Ça c'est bon, chère?"* and Lindsey would giggle and say, *"Ouais,"* in a slow, deep voice like her grandfather's. *"Ouuuaaais, c'est bon."* Finally, when Lindsey had finished all three donuts, he slapped his knees and rose. "It's a pretty little trailer you got," he said.

"You want a tour?" Kay said.

"Next time, maybe."

As his truck backed out of the driveway, Lindsey and Kay both stood at the door, watching him leave.

★   ★   ★

But they didn't go to mass at all. All day, Lindsey read and talked to herself alone in her room and then sat out front on the tongue of the trailer staring at the neighbor's golden retriever as it paced the length of its rope. Finally, at a little before six, she came to Kay and said, "Should we get ready for church?"

Kay, having mowed her little bit of lawn and cooked a casserole that would last most of the week, was sitting at the kitchen table, gnawing her fingernails idly and enjoying the freedom not to do the dishes immediately. "Do you really want to go to church?" she said with some amazement.

"I don't know."

"We can go if you really want to."

They looked at each other, each trying to read in the other's eyes and twist of mouth what role she was meant to play in this conversation.

"I don't know," Lindsey said again. She pivoted on the ball of one foot in a clumsy pirouette, then dropped to one knee and laid both hands on Kay's thigh. "Can we go to Paw Paw's?" she said, bright-eyed.

They did not go to Paw Paw's. But because it would be just like her sisters to come all the way out here to check if they had indeed gone to mass, Kay got Lindsey into the car, vacated the driveway, and drove around aimlessly for an hour instead, down the main drag in Lake Charles, down toward the lake, across the bridge, and into Sulphur, then Moss Bluff, where Kay turned onto a gravel road she had not taken in years. The road skirted the wide, brown Calcasieu River, and Kay followed it for two rattling miles.

Lindsey, on the river side of the car in the front passenger seat (because as long as they were breaking bad, what the hell?), had stopped asking where they were going, and now she leaned against her door, sullen, breathing a fog onto the window and drawing faces in it with the tip of her finger. Kay pointed out any sign of wildlife—egret, turtle, squirrel, barking Labrador—but Lindsey perked up only when they caught the tail of an alligator slipping down into the water. On the other side of the road, Kay's side, stretched a sparse row of rickety camps, mostly old trailers up on stilts, some nicer than others, and a couple of proper houses, also raised at least ten feet, with speedboats parked underneath. Kay kept a close eye on the odometer, and at two miles she looked for familiar landmarks: a pair of date palms at the edge of the road, a sagging concrete wharf carpeted with cypress needles.

The clock on the dashboard clicked over to 7:00, and Lindsey said, "Can we go home now?"

Kay slowed nearly to a stop. The camp, raised high on fifteen-foot pilings, was as she remembered it, except that it was now painted white instead of a deep, rusty red, and had become even more ramshackle. Mildew scaled the clapboard sides. For some reason, a defunct hot tub had been plunked into the yard near the steps leading up to the front door, and now it seemed to serve as a decorative pond of sorts, filled with algae-green water. A clump of water lilies blossomed in its center. A different truck than the one Kay remembered was parked under the house. Though she couldn't be entirely sure the house was still his, she had periodically checked his phone-book listing over the years and always it was marked with this address.

"Who lives there?" said Lindsey.

"I don't know," Kay said. "No one you know. But isn't it interesting?"

The front door swung open, and she might not have recognized him—his hair had grown long and was streaked with some gray, he'd put on weight—except for the bouncing, jaunty gait that brought him down the stairs and into the yard. He raised a hand reflexively to wave at the slow-passing car, and then he disappeared under the house, behind a tower of wooden pallets scavenged from who knows where and being put to who knows what purpose. He'd always had some project going.

On the day she told him she was pregnant, he had been running a haphazard series of tests on a microwave egg-cooker of his own design. One egg after another exploded in a sudden spatter across the microwave window, and when finally, finally, one of them survived to a hard-boiled state, Kay took advantage of his triumphant mood.

"I'm pregnant," she said, and he picked up the boiled egg and flung it. She ducked and it slapped the wall behind her.

"Is it mine?" he asked, so fiercely that Kay was afraid to say.

"I don't know," she said, but she meant it like she'd always said it to her mother when accused of some embarrassing thing—*Kay, did you wet this bed again? What do you mean you don't know?*—just to get out of it, to take it back. She hadn't been with any other man. She didn't mean it like that. Even so, when Nason told her not to ever come back, she didn't

45

argue. Would it even have mattered if she had said yes, the child was his?

Strange to think that of all the men Kay had brought home to her father's house—usually old friends from high school who wouldn't kiss her—her father had only ever approved of the one who'd gotten her pregnant, a man thirteen years her senior who had always been polite but taciturn with her family, eager to flee their presence. Even after Nason sent Kay away, pregnant and crying, Kay's father never said a word against him. As though any betrayals and cruelties perpetrated upon her, especially by a man who by all evidence had his life pretty well in hand, made a good living as a machinist at the plant, and took decent care of a daughter when he had her on weekends, were almost certainly deserved.

Perhaps there should be little surprise that after Nason, Kay had never managed anything like a relationship. Had, in all these years, gone to bed with any of the men she'd dated only a few times before things fell apart. Had, after a while, all but given up. Yet now that she was moved out from her father's house, and her new neighbor in the trailer across the road turned out to be a handsome-ish, young-ish, single-ish man—he was separated from a wife who was, of course, according to him, a bitch and a shrew—Kay thought, *Why not talk to him?*

One Saturday afternoon they sat for a while in his driveway, side by side in lawn chairs, while Lindsey threw sticks and chased and was chased by his floppy, gleeful golden retriever. After a couple of hours, when Lindsey started shoving the dog away and whining that she was hungry, Kay figured what the hell, why not invite the man to join them for dinner?

It was perfectly innocent the way they sat together in the living room after their quick bowl of pasta. He kept to his side of the couch but spread his legs out before him, reclining deeply into the cushions as though he were in his own home. For a while, Lindsey fidgeted between them on the couch, where Kay had directed her to sit while the neighbor tried to draw her out with questions about school, with stories from books he'd read or about places he'd been. He had once been a pilot, he claimed, and in a small plane he'd had to ferry a corpse to another city for burial, and as the plane gained altitude and the air pressure changed in the cabin, the corpse, he swore, had sat up and moaned.

Lindsey, unimpressed, responded in monosyllables and considered her feet. Then she wriggled out from between her mother and the neighbor and moved to the floor, where she had left a coloring book and crayons.

The man also told about the trip he had taken the previous year to Indonesia, as a missionary with his Baptist church, to distribute T-shirts and baseball caps and pamphlets to the little Indonesian kids, and how they lined up for that stuff, were so very polite, not like kids here in the U.S., who just didn't appreciate what they had, etc.

Kay, who had never been anywhere, was anxious that she should add something, or else why would this man who had been places, seen things, care to continue to speak to her, a woman who had been nowhere, seen nothing? "There's a little Indian girl in Lindsey's class." She reached over and tapped the top of Lindsey's head. "What's your little Indian friend called, baby?"

Lindsey whirled on her as though she'd interrupted not the choosing of a crayon but the calibration of a delicate instrument. "She's from Pakistan. Her name is Ayesha."

"You don't have to snap at me."

"Should you talk to your mother that way?" the neighbor said.

"I don't think she should," Kay said. "Have you cleaned your room? I want you to go clean that room, right now."

Lindsey cast a hateful glare upon this man, gathered up her crayons and coloring book, and retreated to her end of the house.

Kay heard the bath running, the bathroom door closing. She apologized on behalf of her daughter. Then she asked the neighbor if he wanted to watch a little television. He did. Kay liked this man. Or, she liked him fine. Why not like him?

After the six o'clock news, a distressing movie about a child gone missing in a shopping mall came on, and Kay and her not unhandsome neighbor scooted perceptibly closer to each other. The TV cast the room's only light. Kay became tinglingly aware of the man's breathing, which had gotten louder, heavier.

Then there was a knock at the door. It was Kay's sisters, backlit by headlights. Her father sat at the wheel of his car in her driveway. He made eye contact with her through the windshield, gave a little wave, then lit a cigarette and stared with disinterest into the dark yard.

When Kay asked what they were doing here, her older

sister told her that Lindsey had called them to say she was scared. "Daddy wanted to come get her." Fleda offered an apologetic eye roll, but her younger sister Beryl was in earnest. After spotting the neighbor man sprawled all over the couch, Beryl tucked her chin into her neck and puckered her tiny resentful mouth. This was the face of someone who, despite her affection for Lindsey, had never forgiven Kay for bringing into the house a baby to unseat her as the youngest, the perpetual child.

"Scared of what?" Kay said.

"She just said *scared*."

Now Lindsey appeared at the door in her pajamas, look-ing about as forlorn as any child could. You'd have thought Kay had abandoned her on a hillside.

Beryl said, "Do you want to come spend the night with us, baby?"

Lindsey did an excited little hop. She pushed past Kay to get to her aunts and squeezed herself between them. Her father flashed the headlights, like *Hurry up*.

To fight this turn of events would require a showdown with her father and sisters, and Lindsey would weep all the way through—a humiliation in front of her male visitor. Plus, in a way that Kay had not anticipated, she was lonelier in this new house with Lindsey there than she was alone. Every time Lindsey shrank from her touch or refused her food or closed the bedroom door against her, Kay was reminded that she was a mother in name only. Even from her own daughter, whom she loved in the most gut-wrenching way, who was her "heart and eyes," as she liked to tell anyone who asked, she could not expect the kind of unconditional love that she herself had to offer and that—although she could hardly admit it to herself—she had expected as part of the bargain and reward for the sacrifice of raising a child on her own. Instead, every bit of her daughter's love went to these people, Kay's family, who had given up nothing for Lindsey's sake, who would shove her away when they were tired of reciting the same rhyme fifty times or when her diaper was dirty or when they had excited her to the point of body-flinging hysterics and could not settle her down. Did most of their paychecks go to her upkeep? Were they the ones who taught her to be polite to strangers and scolded her when she was rude? It wasn't fair. It wasn't right. Not one bit.

But fine, let her go. Kay was tired of fighting it.

After the neighbor left early, claiming he was tired and had work the next day—though the next day was, suspiciously, Sunday—Kay went to the kitchen for two large garbage bags. The angry *pop* of their unfurling echoed through the empty house. Lindsey's room was an epic mess, and though she had been told countless times to clean it, of course she had not. The floor was littered with drawn-on papers, open books, dirty socks. Stuffed animals slumped around an abandoned card game like drunken gamblers at a blackjack table. Kay unhooked her daughter's phone from the wall, wrapped it up in its cord, and chucked it in one of the bags. She picked up every stuffed animal that was out of place and chucked those in the bags too. Every scrap of paper, every book, every sock, the deck of cards. The bed was unmade, so she stripped it and shoved the sheets into the trash bags too. On the dresser lay a letter that Lindsey had started to her older aunt. Kay didn't even want to know what it said. She made an effort not to wrinkle it, but this too went into the bag. It wasn't her intention to throw out her daughter's things. She hoped the threat alone would be enough.

The next morning, when she picked Lindsey up, she said, "You didn't clean your room yesterday like I asked."

Lindsey was quiet. She pressed the button that worked the window all the way down and then all the way up, then all the way down again.

"You know what's going to happen to all that stuff you don't put away? It's going right to the street in plastic bags. You hear?"

"No!" Lindsey said.

"Unless you tell me you're going to start doing what I ask."

"I'll clean. I promise. As soon as we get home."

"And another thing. You weren't very polite to our neighbor yesterday."

Again, Lindsey worked the window, up and down, up and down.

"Did you hear me?"

"So? He's not my father."

Kay almost missed a stop sign and now the nose of her car was poking into the intersection. A driver blared his horn and swerved. "No, he's not. You're right about that." She checked left and right and drove on through, locked the windows so Lindsey couldn't play with them anymore.

Lindsey started kicking her feet against the glove box, leaving footprints on the clean vinyl.

"Do you want to meet your father?" Kay said.

"What?"

"Do you want to meet him? Let's go meet him right now."

Kay took a sudden right into traffic, cutting off a truck that had to slam on its brakes behind her. Again she drove Lindsey over the bridge, through Sulphur and Moss Bluff, down that long gravel road skirting the river.

"Remember this?" she said.

Lindsey's lip was trembling now. As they rattled down the road, folks sitting out on their porches lifted their hands to wave, and Kay waved back, just a finger lifted off the wheel, which she gripped with shaking hands. Then the familiar date palms came into view and Kay swung the car into the driveway, right behind his truck. When she turned the ignition switch, the ticking engine and cottony quiet nearly changed her mind. But she opened her door.

"Come on," she said.

To her surprise, Lindsey followed. They climbed the stairs up to the house and Kay hesitated, then knocked. Lindsey cupped her hands around her eyes and peered through a window. When there was no answer, Kay knocked again. A rattle of tools and metal came from under the house. Lindsey threw herself away from the window and whirled around.

"Hello," the man said. He looked up at them from the foot of the stairs, a hand over his eyes to block the sun.

"Nason?" Kay said.

He started climbing the stairs and about halfway up, he realized who she was. "Well! It's been a long time," he said, as though nothing had passed between them but time. "Y'all come in and visit for a minute, but you got to excuse the state of my clothes." He was in mud-caked hip boots, his denim shirt open around his broad, bald belly, his hair pulled into a ponytail at the nape of his neck. He was a mess, but it was remarkable, really, the way his round cheeks and glinting eyes mirrored Lindsey's.

Kay pushed her daughter in through the open door and he tossed aside a stack of newspapers so they could have a seat on the couch. Nason sat across from them in the recliner, making small talk, then offered them Cokes and asked if they'd mind if he had a beer. Kay said she'd have one too. She drank it fast and he gave her another. Never mind it was only 10 a.m.

He asked Lindsey's name, what grade she was in, asked after Kay's father, sisters, brother. Lindsey sipped her Coke and answered too quietly when he addressed her. When he caught her staring at the picture that hung behind his chair—of another round-cheeked, long-haired girl, this one in a graduation cap—he said, "That's my daughter, Lois. She's at LSU."

"She was just this big last time I saw her," Kay said, and showed how big with her hand. Then, finally, two fast beers in and no breakfast, she caught her nerve. "You know, Nason," she said, "Lindsey is yours too."

Lindsey stiffened. Her fingers made a little dent in the Coke can.

"No, I don't believe so," he said, like she'd asked whether he'd heard a new pop song on the radio.

"You don't have to believe so. It's just true."

"Well, it's the first I've heard it." Nason pointed at Lindsey from his seat in the recliner. "Young lady," he said, "I don't mean any disrespect, but your mother is mistaken on this point. What is it you want, Kay? You want something from me?"

Lindsey started whimpering and Kay threw an arm around her shoulders. "I don't want a thing from you."

"Now, I don't see any need to cry over it," Nason said.

"I don't feel good," Lindsey rasped. "Can we go? Can we please go?"

"I figured you were going to be like this," Kay spat at Nason. She rose from the couch and pulled Lindsey after her.

"Don't go home thinking I made you cry, hon," he said to Lindsey. "It was your momma that brought you here. I didn't have a thing to do with it." And then to Kay, in earnest: "She doesn't deserve that. Look at her. Shame on you."

By the time they made it to the car and locked themselves in, Lindsey was gasping, shaking, her face a crumple of grief. Nason stood at the top of the stairs, watching impassively. Lindsey hinged forward in the seat and clutched her belly.

"Baby," Kay said and touched her back. "Baby, come here."

Lindsey looked at her, glassy-eyed, then threw herself on her mother's chest; she heaved and coughed with weeping. Her tears made a warm, wet spot on Kay's shoulder. "Momma," she wailed. "Momma, momma."

Shame on you, Kay thought, and pulled her daughter closer.

The Ranger Queen of Sulphur

It was nearly dawn, and Deana had been up all night disbanding a cult of hooded dwarves who were sacrificing children to a giant eyeball. Her mouth was dry, her vision fuzzy. There was a tinny hum in her head. But she decided that as long as she was awake anyway, she might as well do as she'd promised and go with her brother to his eight o'clock appointment at the obesity specialist. With at least an hour before she had to leave the house, she packed another bowl into her pipe. She opened her bedroom window, perched the box fan facing outward on the sill, and lit another stick of sandalwood incense, which she sank into the barren dirt of the flowerpot on her cluttered desk. She hit the bowl. She clicked the mouse.

There was plenty of time yet to seek out a curative potion for her druid, who had been struck by a poisoned arrow and was hemorrhaging massive hit points each turn.

Whenever the poison took its toll, the little druid avatar—a long-haired, leather-clad figure with a wooden staff—would shudder and go "Hunh!" In five turns, he would be dead. Azama (née Deana), exiled ranger queen, halted her party in a circle of stone ruins and cast a healing spell on her afflicted companion. It was only a palliative, but it would buy them some time.

"Hunh!" said the druid, and shuddered.

From the dark beyond the ruins emerged a specter in a purple shroud, its hand held up as if in blessing. There was a bright flash. The trees, the stream, the adventurers—all went eerily still. The specter, moving fast, came to the frozen figures each in turn and touched them with its thin fingers. One after another they silently died, last of all the ranger queen. Now on the screen a human hand floated in a starry cosmos. It turned and stretched its fingers as though its owner were regarding it in wonder. With a spasm, the hand exploded into dust. The game blinked off and Deana found herself looking instead at the typing tutorial she had left open the previous night.

"The fuck?" she said. The timer on the ten-key numeric test was still running, nine hours and thirty-seven minutes later.

Granted, she was stoned and therefore apt to overlook or misinterpret vital details, but a lengthy search through her hard drive revealed no evidence of the game file that represented more than four hundred hours of her life for the last four months—about twice what she'd spent at work, and fifteen times what she'd spent on her classes at the vocational college.

It took another long while (just under three minutes, according to the typing timer) of watching a red ember burn the incense stick to ash before she began to understand the magnificence of this loss. All of it, she thought, just gone.

More time gone getting dressed, changing clothes again and again, trying to like this body she had inherited from her father and shared with her brother, this imposing colossus that stood five feet eleven with shoulders like a linebacker's, this mighty frame that—despite breasts for which she had to special-order brassieres—looked ridiculous, she thought, in dresses and in most women's clothes. Fine, so clothe it in jeans, a crew-neck T. Why fuss over what cannot be helped? Although she was large, yes, dense and big of bone, unlike her brother she was not obese; her body, she thought in her best moments, was the body of a warrior. Her best moments, unfortunately, were few.

She had written the information about Jonathan's appointment around the edges of a pay stub and stashed it somewhere not obvious, not on her desk, not in her wallet. Finally she found it on her dresser, under bras and Coke cans. When she pulled it from the mess, she started an avalanche. She kicked aside the towel that was blocking the crack under her door and gave her shoes a twice-over on the way out, once to see if they were tied (they were) and once more because by the time she looked up, she'd already forgotten whether they were or not.

And she was almost on her way.

Her mother was in the kitchen stirring a pot of roux on the stove, easing the bubbling flour-and-oil brew from pasty beige to nearly black. It filled the house with a charred, ashy tang that smelled both catastrophic and delicious. "I've got the ladies for lunch," she said. The ladies being a set of pouf-haired old dames from the local Knights of Columbus hall who invaded each other's homes once a week to confer over crime maps and recipes, to worry each other into a state of panic over cholesterol, and to ask humbling questions of whatever adult children still occupied rooms that should by now have been converted into arts-and-crafts or computer retreats for their retired parents. Deana's mother waved a dish towel like a fan to drive off a hot flash. Her eyes, behind the fogged-up lenses of her glasses, were distressed. "What do you smell like?"

"I don't know. A billy goat? A puppy dog?"

"I really wish you wouldn't burn incense. It's hard on your daddy's lungs. Are you going to the doctor with Jonathan?"

"Well, I told him I would."

"Don't let him agree to anything expensive, he still doesn't have insurance. Here, I want you to bring him some of this." Into a plastic pitcher Deana's mother poured a murky, brown liquid from the jar that had been sitting atop the fridge for weeks with a gray fungus thick as a pancake floating on its surface. She had doted on this concoction, guarded it nervously, so difficult had it been to get her hands on the mushroom—the "mother fungus," she called it—originally obtained from who knows what witch doctor and reputed to work as, among other things, a decongestant, anti-biotic, digestive aid, energy booster, stress buster, weight-loss supplement, hair thickener, rust remover, and foot soak.

"I'm telling you," Deana said, "he's not going to drink that."

"You tell him I said he better. He needs to do something or he's going to end up like Paw-Paw Curtis." She covered the mouth of the pitcher with a layer of plastic wrap. Then she poured more tea into a mug and said, "Go give that to your father."

Deana's father, a six-foot-five Goliath tethered to his recliner by oxygen tubes that snaked from his nose to a humming generator on the floor, sat watching television in the living room. Above his chair a trio of trophies—deer heads with nappy fur and ponderous antlers—hung alongside the bow that had killed them, back in the days when he could breathe. Since then he had fallen under evil enchantment: toxic rags, brought home in the pockets of toxic work clothes, invisibly powdered with dust from the Plant, which Deana, as a little girl, had thought was an actual plant, leafy and noxious, that her father spent his days pruning and watering. "Those work rags," her mother would say, telling the story for the five hundredth time. "I shook them out in the yard where the kids were playing. Nobody told us not to. I threw them in the wash with everything else."

"Mom wants you to drink this."

Her father reached up through the network of tubes and took the mug. He rasped between short, sudden breaths: "Is this that foul potion she's been. Brewing in the jar? That woman is trying. To poison me." He sniffed it, took a sip, and made a little noise of surprise and delight.

"Is it good?" she said.

"Not bad!"

As Deana turned to leave, he grabbed her forearm and looked at her with pleading eyes, his mouth a pucker beneath the cannula moustache. "Boo, catch me that. Remote control. If I have to watch. Another. *Andy Griffith*. I'm gonna shut this machine off. And die."

On her way to the hospital, still high, Deana imagined liposuction too vividly and knew she was going to have to ditch her brother's appointment. Just last week she'd seen the procedure documented on TV in troubling detail: the tube laced through a hole in the flesh, the slurping, slapping, wet sound as it jabbed and sucked at the curdy fat and siphoned it, yellow and blood-marbled, into a jar. She could not possibly sit next to Jonathan while a doctor described such things. And besides, she was nearly late.

She stopped at a green light. The car behind her honked. She took a left and drove east on the long stretch of road that was Sulphur's main drag. She passed car dealerships, trailer dealerships, dollar stores, and the cross street that led to the hospital. She passed the Payday Loan where she spent most afternoons. After two miles through tank farms and a sloppy complex of hotels and floating casinos, she crossed the bridge to Lake Charles and pulled off, finally, at the beach.

She backed her truck across the sand, lowered the tailgate, and stretched belly-down on the rusted bed. Greenish foam washed up at the shoreline and congealed. On the opposite shore: a petrochemical metropolis, the likely source of this muck. Vista, Olin, City Services. A long white burn-off cloud trailed from a smokestack to join a low blanket of actual clouds, which made it seem the plants and refineries might be the source of all weather and gloom. If Deana had some magic thing of power—a ring of PVC pipe forged in the fires of Vista Chemical, say—she might breach that dark city, sneak past the guards and alarms, and chuck the ring into a vat of boiling liquid plastic. The whole place would be consumed in its own evil flames. All would bow to the heroine who had broken the poisonous magic: Deana LaFleur, Ranger Queen of Sulphur.

But she was only who she was: a girl who had twice been held back in middle school, having sopped up the bleak conviction that all roads lead to Kmart or the Plant, so why bother? A girl upon whom, at twenty-five, it was only now starting to dawn that certain basic occupational skills might at least rescue her from the lowest forms of drudgery, but who, true to her nature, skipped three of every four classes. In fact, she had a typing class later that morning. Would she go? Probably not.

Beyond the tailgate the foul-breathed water kissed the shore. Down the beach, a pair of young men had turned up with a four-wheeler and were skidding out across the sand, shouting. A rebel flag streamed behind them.

"Assholes," Deana said. Then she stood up in the bed of her truck and yelled it: "Assholes! Assholes!" But clearly they couldn't hear her.

Jonathan lived in a rental house on Eighteenth Street, in a neighborhood of lonely old ladies and young black families, and thus of cheaper rents and greater freedom to, say, rescue as many greyhounds as he cared to from the track at Delta Downs. So far he had cared to rescue three. The dogs, in varying stages of obesity themselves, ran barking to Deana when she opened the gate, the oldest a stout barrel on spindly legs, the youngest still slim and spry but for arthritic ankles wrapped tightly in gauze. The middle dog leaped up and pushed at her chest with its front paws. She raised the pitcher of tea above her head. "Call off your hounds," she said.

Jonathan sulked in the open doorway. He had to turn himself at an angle to get through. "Why should I?"

"Sorry I missed your appointment," she said, and didn't feel sorry at all, only angry that she should put up with so much and get no sympathy for her own failings.

"Whatever," said Jonathan. He pointed at the jumping dog. "Just knee her in the chest when she does that. Ruthie, down!"

Deana held out the pitcher. "Mother sent you mushroom tea."

"Ew."

"She said if you don't drink it, you'll turn into Paw-Paw Curtis."

"I liked Paw-Paw Curtis."

"I just remember he had no feet."

Jonathan took the pitcher and waddled toward the kitchen. A Big Gulp cup was sweating by the sink, and he popped the lid off and dumped out its watered-down contents. He filled it nearly to the top with the tea, poked the straw in, and snapped down the lid. The youngest dog raised itself, slowly and gracefully, onto hind legs and rested its front paws on the counter. It laid back its ears and twitched its nose.

"Get down," Jonathan said, with no conviction. He swung his hip and bumped the dog to the floor.

"It smells weird in here," Deana said. She shivered, rubbed at the goose bumps on her arms. "And it's freezing."

"So?" Even in the dreadful heat of Louisiana summers, Jonathan wore full-length pants that covered, but did not hide, the grotesqueries that were his legs. His stomach, a thick, drooping apron that hung down to his thighs, was bunched in the voluminous crotch of his pants and swayed when he walked, the great shuffling mass of him bumping walls and rattling the house as he went. He had never, ever been thin, but there had been a time, in his teens and early twenties, when he might have passed as "a big guy" like Deana was "a big girl," with the kind of bulky physique that straddled the line between might and fat. Even then, he had been sensitive about it. Once, when he was twenty-four, still living at home and soon to abandon pursuit of the world-religions degree he had been slowly creeping up on at the local college for seven years, Deana, only thirteen, told him giddily that he looked—with his Coke-bottle glasses and greasy black hair—exactly like her then-hero, Stephen King. She'd thought this was a compliment, but he slapped shut the textbook he was reading and threw it so hard across the room it left a dent in the wall. "And what do you think *you* look like, you mean little bitch?"

Now, Deana sat astride the arm of the sofa, wanting to make clear that she had no intention to stay and get high. For one thing, she couldn't bear the smell of these dogs. The newest one leaped onto the sofa and curled up, pressed against her leg. It sighed. Jonathan sat down next to it—the cushions under the dog rising up in a little hill, displaced by Jonathan's great weight—and patted its rump. He took a few tiny, quick sips from his giant cup of mushroom tea.

"What did the doctor tell you?" Deana said.

"He said lap-band surgery would be a good option." He set the cup on the floor and started loading the bowl of a pretty little glass pipe.

"Lap band? What is that?"

"They put, like, a rubber donut around your stomach to make you feel full."

"Fuck."

"And if you eat too much, you have 'productive burping.'"

"You mean you throw up?"

"It's 'productive burping.'"

"Gross."

Jonathan took a long draw off the pipe and held his breath. Through the exhale he said, "I guess it works really well. He's known people who lost, like, over two hundred pounds. But the surgery's too expensive."

"How expensive?"

"Twenty-five thousand dollars. So, you know, fuck it. I'll just be fat."

"Um," said Deana. "Why don't you not eat?"

"I wish you would stop asking me that."

"Go back to OA, then."

"Those bitches are assholes."

He passed Deana the pipe and a lighter, and in spite of her best intentions, she took it. She poked the dog until it moved from the couch, and then she settled into the cushions next to her brother. Before she took a hit, she let herself relish just the slightest hint of clear-minded outrage at this brother who would do nothing for himself, who could just relax into his misery, accept his imprisonment. At least, Deana thought, *she* was learning to type.

"Well, it's not like you're a shut-in yet, I guess." She set fire to the bowl.

Jonathan rocked himself out of his seat and went to the cassette tapes stacked two rows deep in towers on the bookshelf, their cases cracked and yellowed. He grabbed too many at a time and held them to his chest, picked through them one by one, examining the labels, many of them home-recorded, inscribed in the handwriting of high school and college friends who had, as far as Deana knew, long ago fled Sulphur. At last he found the one he wanted and shoved the rest back onto the shelf. "I'm digging the Bad Brains lately again," he said.

While the first song rushed from the speakers, beat its chest, bared its fangs, Jonathan shuffled to the kitchen and returned with a container of vanilla icing, a spoon, and a bowl of broccoli florets drizzled with white dressing. He took his place on the couch and balanced these things on his lap and knees, alternating crunchy florets with heaping white spoonfuls of frosting.

"Oh my God, Jonathan," Deana yelled over the pounding bass. "What are you eating?"

"Fuck off."

For the length of the cassette, they sat together on the couch in silence. The dogs, hypnotized by the prospect of food, stood frozen before Jonathan, noses to the carpet, ears alert, waiting for something to drop. When Deana was roused from her stupor by a shaking—rhythmic, constant—of the couch, she turned to her brother and saw him jerking his shoulders, wagging his head, twitching his feet. Somehow he danced under the weight of his weight like he could shake this body off, wriggle out as the thin punk-rock Jonathan who'd been sheltered there all this time.

He knocked the bowl of broccoli to the floor and the dogs lunged. They licked the splattered dressing from each other's paws, from the carpet, from the couch. They bumped each other's thick bodies out of the way and, in their clumsy chaos, toppled the Big Gulp cup. A puddle of mushroom tea spread across the rug. Jonathan gazed calmly upon the mess at his feet, sighed, and scooped up another helping of icing.

Deana stretched out her hand. "Give me some of that."

"Watch out, Dee," he said. "The dread serpent will come for you too."

At the Payday Loan, Deana sat at a desk behind bulletproof glass. Almost always—for the first few hours anyway, before the five-o'clock rush—she was unsupervised and alone. She was equipped at her station with a creaky oscillating chair, the cash drawer, a telephone, and, most important, a computer with an online connection for recording transactions, looking up payment history, and, when no one was watching, searching whatever idle phrases came into her head, like *get me out of here* (about 1,340,000 hits) and *I hate Sulphur* (ten hits, eight relevant: "I hate Sulphur, LA, it's a flipping black hole" et al.; two more, not relevant: one by a blogger with a special loathing for sulphur-crested cockatoos and the other by a frustrated chemistry student). Today, Deana positioned her fingers on the keys as the typing teacher had shown her and gradually entered into the search engine the phrase *lap band surgery*.

If the first several links gave the same information, albeit in far more sophisticated and detailed terms, that Jonathan had already given her, the last link on the page was a revelation. Apparently this surgery, so expensive in America, could be performed for a fraction of the cost—only about forty-five hundred dollars in fact, a hefty but not unreasonable sum—in Mexico. There was a form on the website for scheduling consultations. Profound changes were as simple as clicking SUBMIT.

Moreover, when Deana opened another search screen and, surrendering the unattainable ideal of ten-finger typing, picked out with one finger the phrase *border crossing Mexico,* she found that it was no big trick to just *go* there. Mexico had always seemed as impossibly distant to her as New York or China, the only realistic destinations from the departure point of Sulphur being New Orleans, Houston, and possibly Memphis, these three the frontier outposts on the rim of her map. But with no passport, almost no money, only minimal plans, a person could simply *go.* Remarkable. Even she could maybe manage this.

Someone tapped at the glass of her cashier's window. It was a plump white woman with a lopsided hairdo and a right arm that ended at the elbow. She had first come in five months ago for an advance on her Walmart check and then again two weeks after that, and again two weeks later, and on and on, paying the growing fees and interest but always extending the loan at what was effectively an annual rate of over 3,000 percent. Deana had cashed her checks, minus the fees, and shoved back through the slot in the window an ever-diminishing pittance of bills and change, less than fifty dollars last time, with which this woman must somehow feed, clothe, and house herself for the next two weeks. Then the woman had stopped coming in. The catastrophe that began this miserable cycle—what could it have been? a busted refrigerator, a loss on the dogs, bail for an over-loved son?—now months distant. One crisis exchanged for another.

Sad. Well, what could Deana do? She probably got disability, at least.

"Somebody's been calling my workplace threatening to have me arrested."

"I'm not the one calling, ma'am."

"Well, who is?"

"Probably my manager. But he isn't here." Deana asked for the woman's name and pulled up her file on the computer, making a show of doing something when she already knew there was nothing to be done. She said blandly, "It says you owe $620.75 and you haven't made a payment since February. That's why you're getting calls."

"Six hundred twenty dollars? For a two-hundred-dollar loan?" Her voice was tearful, plaintive, infuriating. "How am I supposed to pay that back?"

"I'm sorry but," Deana recited, as she had been trained to do, "you were given the terms of the loan and you signed a contract. If you fail to pay, we can report you to a collection agency. We can file charges of bank fraud, and"—she always fumbled over this blatant untruth—"we can have you arrested." Like most of the sad sacks who came in, this woman didn't know any better, and setting her straight was not Deana's job. She'd nearly been fired for that before.

The woman slid her purse from her shoulder and pinned it against her chest with the nubby right arm. The purse's strap was wrapped completely in duct tape and it flopped over the half arm while she rooted around. Finally she produced a wadded-up bill. "I can give you twenty right now, and when I get my next check, I'll give you another fifty."

This too was a dead end. "We can't take partial payments unless you give us your checking-account number."

"I don't have a checking account."

"So you have to pay in full."

The woman tried to push the crumpled twenty through the slot, but Deana blocked the opening with her hand.

"You're telling me you won't take my money?" The woman turned to a young black man who had come in after her. A very small girl was pressed against his leg and held on to his fingers with both hands. "I don't understand why nobody will help me," the woman shrilled. "I can barely even buy my groceries. Young lady, why won't you help me?" Trembling with rage, the woman delivered to the young man and the little girl and the echoing walls of the otherwise-empty storefront a disjointed tirade about Christian charity and a dying cat and a leaking roof and her own missing arm.

"They're thieves," the man said, and looked squarely at Deana. "They don't care about nothing or nobody." Then he picked up his little girl, propped her on his hip, and went on his own tirade. Electric bill. Surgery. Denied unemployment benefits. On and on. "Usury is a sin," he said. "It's a sin!"

Deana rose from her chair and pretended to search for something in a filing cabinet, her back to the window. After all, he was right. She didn't care. Let these people learn to read a contract. Let this woman not have lost an arm. Let them have been born somewhere else, as someone else, or not at all.

"You should be ashamed," the woman said to Deana's back, and left the store.

When Deana had processed the man's transaction and was once again alone, she came from behind the wall of her station and stood at the storefront door, gazing out. It was midafternoon. There was a heavy quiet on the main drag. Now and then a car crept by, fairly tiptoed. Deana locked the door, turned off the lights, and lay on her back right there in the entryway, the widest, emptiest patch of linoleum in the store. She stretched out her arms and legs. The fluorescent light above her was the saddest thing she'd ever seen.

Later that night, in the customer-service booth of the Kroger, Deana squatted on a footstool that Jonathan had been using to elevate his ashy gray feet, freed of their shoes but concealed from customers by a wall that enclosed the office from which Jonathan, once ensconced for his evening shift, was rarely called upon to descend. Split open in his hands was a raggedy novel with a snarling, bloodied pair of Dobermans on the cover. He put it aside reluctantly.

Deana shuffled through papers she'd printed from the internet and explained about the doctor in Reynosa, just across the Rio Grande from McAllen, Texas—practically still the United States, really, and only eight hours away. "Americans go there all the time for prescriptions. It's so freaking cheap," she said. "You could just put it on your credit card."

Jonathan said, "Why is it so cheap?"

"I don't know. It's Mexico. You have a consultation next week." She showed him reviews, testimonials, before-and-after photos, the doctor's credentials—which were, granted, Mexican, their credibility impossible to assess. But there was a photo of this doctor, smiling, mustached, trim and clean in a white coat, posing with a smiling patient. She said, "We've got to do something."

A pair of eyes peeked over the tall counter of the booth. "Excuse me?" said a woman. "Excuse me?"

Jonathan swiveled his chair to face her.

"Do y'all—" she said, sticking a little on the *y'all,* "do *y'all* have wonton wrappers?"

"Wonton wrappers?" said Jonathan.

"You use them to make egg rolls," the woman said. She looked from Jonathan to Deana. "It's the wrapper." She swirled a finger. "Around the egg roll."

"I know what they are," Jonathan said. He picked up the intercom mic but put it back down when he saw the long, curling lines at the registers, only two open—the late-night shift. "Just a minute," he said, and leaned sideways to retrieve his shoes from where they were tucked under the desk with his socks stuffed inside them. He took a sock in hand, scrunched it down to the toe, and rocked forward, wheezing, until sock met foot. He sat up again, panted for a while, then went for the other one. He did not bother to tie the shoes. "Let's look," he said. He descended the three steps from the service booth, still out of breath and, waving the woman to follow, shuffled off toward the back of the store. The woman went after him in half steps and pauses, trying not to dart rudely ahead of the slow-plodding fat man.

The woman was actually a girl, or not a girl, really, but young, Deana's age or a little younger, and, judging from the accent, not from around here, or from around here but more like one of those kids Deana remembered from high school who talked about college as though it was something they'd actually do, and then, lo and behold, did, who would come back from summers chatting blithely about the house at Holly Beach, fishing the Gulf, or, a few of them, about weed in Amsterdam, punk clubs in Prague, who ran for student government or hung out in the art room making beaded necklaces and marionettes out of papier-mâché, who wrote columns, plays, poems, songs, learned guitar, like they thought anyone actually gave a fuck, like they thought they could actually do something. Like they could march into any damn place and ask for any damn thing they pleased.

"Wonton wrappers," Deana clucked when Jonathan was back in the booth. "Jesus! Where does she think she is?"

His feet came out of the shoes again and he stripped off the socks, which required much the same effort as before. "We usually have them. They're just out of stock." He was gasping for air, sweating through his shirt.

"Jonathan," Deana said. "How can you deal with that every day and not shoot yourself? We can go. Did you know that? We aren't trapped. We can just go."

"So you go, then. Bring me back a sombrero and some Chiclets." He picked up the novel again and held it in front of his face. She kept at him for half an hour, but he wouldn't budge.

★　★　★

They rarely came together as a family, and almost never as a family with other families. She had overheard her mother's excuses on the phone often enough. Jonathan was said to be shy, Deana busy with school. Of course it was always too hard on her father. Saturday was her father's birthday, however, and thus one of those extraordinary occasions that found them all in one place. Deana had not been warned (or had she?) about the gathering that was to take place in their kitchen and so stumbled into it, having just woken up at the indecent hour of noon, still wearing boxers, an oversize T-shirt, and no bra, reeking of weed.

Her father sat at the kitchen table with a store-bought cake in front of him. He was telling a story—one of his great pleasures, though the going was slow—to the husbands of the KC hall ladies. One of the men leaned against the refrigerator and kept checking his feet to see that he was clear of the oxygen tubes. Two more men were cocked back in chairs at the table, while her mother and three other ladies admired the mushroom tea. They passed it among themselves, mirthful with revulsion, and held it up to the light to examine the pale, webby scum that hung in amber liquid at the bottom of the jar. Jonathan teetered on a little stool in a corner far from the others. He was reading, or pretending to read, the local paper. It fell to Deana, as always, to be the presentable child.

Feeling like a lumbering giantess next to these women, nasty in mood and body, she crossed her arms over her bra-less breasts and said, "It's magic. Did Mother tell you? It cures cancer. It relieves debt. I'm pretty sure it summons demons."

Jonathan snorted in the corner, the only sign that he had been listening. The women looked at her like she'd spoken in tongues.

Her mother laughed weakly. "You don't have to make fun."

"Does it really do all that?" one of the women said. They speculated in earnest until an explosion of deep-bellied laughter from the men interrupted them. Her father had finished his story. There was an amiable pause during which they all—men and women—looked from one to the other. Jonathan rustled the newspaper and adjusted his fanny creakily on the stool. The jar of tea had made its way back to Deana's mother. She cradled it in the crook of one arm and said, philosophically and to no one in particular, oblivious to the lull in the room, "I just thought it might be good for Jonathan."

The guests turned their gaze casually to Jonathan, as though genuinely to assess in what sense the tea might be good for him. When he felt them all watching him, he peered over the top of the newspaper, then deliberately folded it and set it aside. If his weight had not pinned him so stubbornly in place, he might have risen and, with dignity, left the room. But then, if such an exit had been possible, he would not have been the subject of this unwelcome attention in the first place. Instead he sat there resting his hands on either side on his enormous belly, face stoic, like a greasy-haired, bespectacled Buddha.

"Well, we're all carrying a little extra around these days," said one of the men.

"You've got to love the body you got, hon," said one of the women.

74

Her father slapped a thigh with exaggerated enthusiasm and said something about the great-looking cake.

But their mother would not drop it. Flustered by her own faux pas, she grew shrill and angry. "It's a matter of health. His grandfather suffered so bad with diabetes. Do you think I want to see my child go through that? Lose his eyesight? Lose his feet? Jonathan, do you want to lose your feet?"

Jonathan was rocking himself back and forth for momentum. At first it looked like he might topple to the floor, but with one hand gripping the countertop and another braced against his thigh he managed to hoist himself off the low stool. Still wearing an impassive expression but sweating now, either from effort or shame, he said, "Don't be ridiculous. The asbestos poisoning will get us first."

Had Jonathan and Deana been alone together, warding off with jokes the dull terror that, in lighter moments, they had come to call, almost affectionately, the Big Suck, Deana would have laughed. But the acerbic, angry fatalism that registered in her mind and her brother's, paradoxically, as a weird kind of optimism did not sound so much like optimism when others were listening too. Her father's oxygen hiss-clicked. The men looked at the table or their shoes. The women looked at her mother, who squirmed as though she had been accused and then removed herself from the room.

And her father—whose good cheer relied not at all on mean tactics and was uncannily, even supernaturally, inexhaustible—he too seemed stricken and suddenly pale. "I don't appreciate that at all," he said.

Jonathan gave a nervous laugh and looked helplessly at Deana. She offered nothing, and finally, without another word, he squeezed past the men and left the room.

The gathering recovered. Soon her mother returned, red-eyed but wearing a calculatedly pleasant face. She served the cake. Deana's father embarked upon another story in which he was a reluctant and humble hero.

When Deana had sat long enough for propriety, she flopped a big slab of cake onto a plate and went after her brother. He was at her computer, playing the game she thought had disappeared from her hard drive. She felt a pang of joy and nostalgia, a dizzy longing for the familial little band of warriors, alive and battling orcs. She set the cake on the desk and watched over her brother's shoulder while he routed the enemy. When the gasps and groans and clanking armor had finally ceased, Jonathan paused the game. "Okay," he said but didn't turn around.

"Okay?"

"Okay." He wobbled his head, a little no, a little yes. "Okay, fine. We'll go to Mexico."

He had conditions, though. They would not tell their parents, or anyone else, about the appointment. If asked, they were driving to Memphis for barbecue. All the way there for barbecue? Yep, all the way there. A weekend of messy, mustardy sauce, and they would come back fatter than ever before. He wanted snacks for the road—Doritos, beef jerky, sacks of bite-size chocolate candies—and a two-day orgy of illicit tasties, truck-stop hot dogs and *taquitos*, fast food for breakfast, lunch, and dinner. All to celebrate his imminent transformation. They spent almost a hundred dollars at Kroger.

The night before they were to leave, after packing her bag, smoking the last of her weed, and answering a call from a woman speaking first Spanish, then English, to confirm the appointment for Jonathan at the clinic in two days, Deana left a message for her brother to be ready at six the next morning. She was eyeing her computer and, having resisted the urge until now, was considering a celebratory binge of her own when her father, detached from his oxygen machine, tapped on her door frame. "Your mother's at keno," he said. "And the Weather Channel says. It's a nice night. How about taking a little ride. Baby doll?"

"Where?"

"I don't know. Anywhere. I ain't been out of this house. In a lifetime."

At night, from the top of the Lake Charles Bridge, the plants dazzled, a spectacle: merry twinkling lights, fires atop chimneys white and slim and tall as dinner candles. The casino boats floated at the shore, yoked to the town like a couple of water buffalo to drag it out of the sludge pit of the 1980s. They rolled down the windows, drove slow over the bridge, turned around and drove back over. She took him to the little beach, parked the truck facing the lake and the lights, and they sat for a while and looked.

"Peanut," he said, "I've been meaning to say. Your mother and me."

She felt a sudden terror that this would be the moment when he would tell her, finally—and it was about time, really—to leave his house and get out on her own, to quit getting high and messing around and squandering the life that he had wasted himself to give her. The oxygen canister, which leaned between them on the seat, released its gas in abrupt, quiet gasps whenever her father took a breath.

"We've been meaning to say," he said at last. "We're proud of you. For going back to school. And for being a good sister. To your brother."

She said nothing and did not look at him.

He reached over and patted her hand, let his fingers rest on hers. "I still know people over there," he said, and she knew he meant that twisted thicket of pipes and tank farms across the lake. "When you get your certificate. I can get you in."

"Okay, Daddy," she said.

"It's fine work, baby doll."

"Okay," she said. Deana withdrew her hand from his.

"Not like it was." The wide lake was spattered with moonlight, casinolight, Plantlight. One of the chimneys at Vista, dormant until now, threw up a hot yellow tongue of flame that sputtered and steadied. Her father took as deep a breath as he could and sighed. "Sometimes it's almost. Pretty."

When Deana pulled into her brother's driveway at six o'clock sharp, his house was dark, the door shut and locked. She knocked for a long time. The dogs barked in a frenzy inside, until finally a light blinked on, they settled down, and her brother, hushing them, squinting, wild-haired, opened the door.

"Why aren't you up?" she said.

He yawned without covering his mouth. His pajamas were sweatpants and the biggest T-shirt she had ever seen. She followed him inside and closed the door, kneed the dogs away from her. She looked at her watch, showed it to him, tapped it. "I told you six. Hurry up!"

"I'm not going," he said. Like *I'm not hungry*. Or *Pass the salt*.

"You're going."

"I can't. There's nobody to watch the dogs." He sat on the couch and lolled his head to one side. The dogs piled on. The whole pack of them, her brother and his greyhounds, were still in their morning moods, just this side of drowse. "God, I'm sleepy," he said. "How are you so perky?"

"You said that guy Wyatt could take them."

"He said no."

"You said he said yes."

"He did. And then he said no."

"Then why don't you leave them at the vet, like everyone else?"

"I can't leave them in those little cages." He rested an arm along the spine of a curled-up dog.

"With Mom and Dad, then."

"Are you joking?"

"Then we'll take them with us. Jonathan, get up!" She grabbed his damp, mushy arm and pulled, but he did not budge. He shook Deana off and tried to cross his legs at the ankles, gave up and spread them wide, sunk low in the cushions and smacked his lips. Again the slow yawn, the squinting eyes. "I'm out of weed," he sighed. "Let's drive to Orange and stock up."

Deana glared at him, astonished. "We bought all that food." It was in her truck right now, in the middle of the bench seat, a fiesta in a cardboard box.

One of the dogs sat up on the sofa to scratch its side, and Jonathan slung an arm around it and pulled it close. He buried his face in the dog's neck and stayed that way for so long Deana thought he must have fallen asleep.

"You're going to get all that shit out of my truck. Right now. Get up."

He did not move.

"Jonathan!"

"Okay, okay."

She held the door open impatiently while he crammed his feet into flip-flops, and when he was finally coming out, she let it slam shut in his face. At the truck she waited again by the open passenger's door. It took him forever to cross the lawn.

"So, Orange later?" he said.

"I have a class."

"What class?"

"A typing class."

"That sucks. Weren't you going to skip it anyway?"

"Not to go to Orange."

"Maybe tomorrow, then." Clutching the box of snacks against his belly, he turned away, as though this delivery had been the sole purpose of her visit all along. The dogs wrestled clumsily under the trees. Jonathan gave a quick whistle. All three bounded into the house and he followed them and shut the door.

★　★　★

She thought by now she might have been dropped from the roster. She expected a scolding at least, but the instructor nodded when she walked in and gestured for her to take a seat at one of the open typewriters. He scanned the list of names on his roll, finally asked her to remind him of hers, and then got immediately on with it. They were learning on typewriters rather than computers, he had explained long ago on the first day of class, because it would make their fingers stronger, the typewriter keys being stickier, more stubborn. But really, most probably, Deana knew, this crappy vocational school could not afford a whole classroom of computers. Typewriters they had, so typewriters it would be.

The other students were a motley range of ages and colors. Her nearest neighbor was a middle-aged black woman in neat, secretarial attire, and on the other side sat a big white kid who could be only just out of high school, with thick, immobile hands that had probably suffered in their attempts at fine-motor activities since the early days of Legos and shoe-lacing. The students rolled paper into their machines and waited. Deana did the same. The teacher began to chant:

A space J space semicolon space

R space U space 7 space 5

cat hat rat bat pat goat moat

Pre-words, nonsense, became one syllable, then two, the words became phrases, the phrases proverbs.

Practice makes perfect.

An ant may well destroy a whole dam.

Better to light a candle than to curse the darkness.

And many of the others clickety-clacked right along, had indeed become nimble or nearly so, even the kid with the

81

impractical hands. Their progress weeks ago had seemed so impossibly, so glacially slow. It felt then, as it felt now, like Deana was accomplishing exactly nothing, going exactly nowhere; that she would never type or drive or toke her way out of this place that pinned her like a boulder on her toe, that could only be named after the stink it produced. It was the plants and the heat and the ruthless mosquitoes, the price of gas, the addictive games, the crappy jobs, the hostile rednecks, hopeless brothers, delinquent cousins, complacent mothers, jobless fathers, spiteful uncles, polluted waters, the stifling reek of sulfur and fast food and tanker-truck exhaust. It was the vague, embedded memory of those desolate '80s, the oil-bust years, the slim Christmases and government-issued "cheese food." The bumper stickers everywhere that read LAST ONE OUT SHUT OFF THE LIGHTS! It was all of this and it was none of this. And if it wasn't this, what was it? It was her. It was in her. It was something awful in her. What candle could light such a darkness?

All around, the slow, tapping drone rose to a crescendo, an orchestra of swiftly clacking keys. And now, still, she could not hit a letter without looking for it first, and when she found it, she jabbed it with the same rage and hate that she might the eyes of a foe.

Poke Salad

Yesterday your old daddy just about checked out. Let me tell you.

There's a song on one of these long plays you sent last year for Christmas. "Poke Salad Annie, gators got your granny," something like that. Well, old Poke Salad Annie and her no-count daddy don't have a thing to eat, so Annie goes out and picks her daddy a mess of greens in what they call a poke sack, which is I believe how the plant got its name—

Now, that song sounds pretty good coming out of those speakers I put together last year. Good sounds! Since your old daddy got retired from the plant, he's got a lot of time to just sit and think. I put on the long plays and watch the boats just easing down the river, and I start to feel sort of romantic. Like old Ishmael. How did old Ishmael put it? "I rejoice in my *spine.*" Whoa.

Whoa! I get thoroughly philosophical with some good sounds, baby doll.

(I know I'm talking your ear off, and I can tell I woke you up, but I forget the time difference, and to tell you the truth, I'm making some pretty good progress on my Heinekens, here. You can't fault your old daddy for that.)

But getting back to poke salad: it grows down here and people do eat it. You can probably find it growing wild out in California, too. Look it up: *P-O-K-E* salad.

Right, like *salad*.

Well, the water went down in that back lot of mine enough that I could get out there in my regular shoes to cut the weeds, and I found this plant that I know is what they're calling poke salad in that song. Seeing it was Thanksgiving, I thought, *I'm going to treat myself.* (I'm telling you, I eat just fine down here, baby. You don't have to worry about that.) I tossed the leaves in a bowl, sprinkled some vinegar. Man. Talk about delicious. It might have been the best mess of greens I've ever consumed. I mean that was an *excellent* salad.

Then old Charlie knocked on the door to bring me a plate of turkey. Now, you must think your old daddy is alone out here on the river, but Charlie, he'll deign to come over sometimes and shoot the shit with the likes of me. He's the one built that monolithic camp next door with the two-story wharf that thoroughly obstructs my peripheral view of the river. Charlie was a regional something-or-other for British Petroleum, so he did all right.

Anyhow, I was neighborly and offered him some of my poke salad. Charlie took one look and said, "Nason, you can't eat that!"

Charlie can be kind of an arrogant outfit. Take for example the time he tried to tell me division by zero did *not* result in infinity, when you and I and Stephen Hawking all know it sure as shit does. Whenever I get contrary, Charlie gives me that look, like I'm just the local color around here.

So I said, "Buddy, I can and will."

He said, "Man, that stuff is poison!"

I said, "The hell you say," and proceeded to eat my poke salad.

After Charlie left, I sat down at the computer—

(Did I tell you I got the internet? The next time you come down, it'll be there for you. I have it in mind that one of these days you'll use this place as a base of operations. You don't have to always stay at your granddad's. You're welcome anytime.

Uh hunh.

Uh *hunh*.

You're saying *Okay,* but I know how your mind works: *Man, I ain't never going to do that.* Let me tell you something: one day I saw a house leaning sideways, and I thought to myself, I'll never live in a house like that. Five years later, I was living in that very house. You don't know what you'll do.)

Anyway, come to find out Charlie was *right*. I've got one word for you, baby: *phytolaccatoxin*. You get enough of that and you're in trouble. "Expect convulsions, prostration." Expect *prostration*! I only had about eight leaves, but before long the undersides of my feeps was tingling. The undersides of my *feeps*! I was sweating through my clothes, I had shortness of breath. I like to not made it to the bathroom, if you know what I'm saying.

When I came to, I was *prostrate,* in the dark, on the bathroom floor. I managed to sort of cock myself to the side on my knee and flip over, but man, that's all I had in me. I thought, *Hell, Nason, what have you done to yourself now?* I looked in the direction of the Lord to say my last prayers, and I'll tell you what I saw, baby. Let me tell you what I saw. Just listen.

I saw a shaft of moonlight coming in through the window over the commode, and spinning in that moonlight, I saw a galaxy. I'm telling you, a *galaxy.* Then one of those palmetto bugs shot across the light like a comet. I heard its wings whirring, that *slap* when it hit the wall.

Fffftttttthhhhhhrrrrrrrrrrr-pock!

And I thought: well, okay. *Okay.*

And that's what I'm calling to tell you.

You can come down here whenever you want, and I'll be happy to have you, even though I know you don't want to be down here when you're down here. And I don't want you down here out of a sense of duty. You got no duty to me. Let me ask you something: Who were those old boys that walked through the flames?

Shadrach, Meshach, and Abednego, that's right. Those old boys walked through fire and they *survived.*

And that's what I'm calling to tell you.

I walked through flames, baby doll, and I *survived.*

The Whiskey Business

Cross-legged on the floor of the foyer in suite 3-J, Janessa presses her sore shoulders to the cinder-block wall and imagines an impassive, bespectacled man—Nabokov, maybe—sticking her wings to a board with pins. Jacqui Watson, one of her suitemates, is telling her and Wei Wei about how, at the Model UN conference in Baton Rouge last weekend, Royce Bright followed their other suitemate, Andrea Garner, into the governor's private bathroom in the capitol and raped her.

"Andrea didn't say *raped*," Jacqui acknowledges. "She said *assaulted*. But that's what she meant."

Andrea told this to her today, Jacqui says, Wednesday, at dinner. Since returning from the trip on Sunday, Andrea has been only as strange as Andrea ever is: picking without appetite at her undressed salads, tugging out her eyelashes, one by one, when she thought no one was looking. Then when she and Jacqui were alone earlier tonight at one of the tables near the cafeteria jukebox, which was probably blasting "Blood Sugar Sex Magik" (as it has been seemingly ever since they came to the Governor's Academy for Science, Arts, and Humanities as juniors, more than a year ago, and likely longer than that), Royce Bright and his crew slapped their trays down at a neighboring table and began sniggering into their Cokes. Aneesh Prajapati, Johnny Zhao, and Norman Sidney Robinson—like Royce—are Lincoln-Douglas-debating, pi-to-the-nth-decimal-reciting dickwads, all narrow-shouldered with the exception of Norman Sidney, who weighs three hundred pounds if he weighs a penny. Andrea forked a clump of lettuce into her mouth and retched it back onto a napkin. At first Jacqui laughed, thinking she was just being a smart-ass about the guys at the next table, but Andrea said it wasn't funny and that's when she told her what happened.

It made sense that she would tell Jacqui, if anyone. Three weeks into the fall semester of last year, Jacqui had lit out naked across the quads in a thunderstorm, shrieking, "The penises! The penises! They're after me!" and, once captured by an RA from Burton, the boys' dorm, had been ushered promptly to her RA on the third floor of Caddo, the girls' dorm, wrapped in blankets, soaked, giggling. The girls' RA, an undergraduate at the college with which their magnet school shares a campus and thus only nominally more adult than the high school students under her supervision, medicated Jacqui with a Twix bar from the lobby vending machine and a Xanax. After that, she was sent back to suite 3-J, the crazy suite full of crazy girls with big tits (Jacqui and Wei Wei), a predilection for computer gaming (Andrea), ethnically indecipherable hair (Jacqui, again), and an honest-to-God hunchback (Janessa).

No one called Jacqui's parents, but the whole school knew it had happened, and the incident gave her a reputation as someone to whom girls could go with anything. Confessions didn't shake her. Neither did she guard them, though, and tonight she tells Andrea's to Janessa and Wei Wei. Andrea herself has not yet come back from the campus computer lab, where she spends most nights until curfew.

"Royce Bright? Of course he did," Wei Wei says, matter-of-fact.

She's been deflecting insults from Royce's compadre Aneesh Prajapati ("Hey, walrus! Shave your moustache!") ever since their aborted tryst behind the hometown mall. She and Aneesh had made out, and then, so Wei Wei told Janessa, he dug his slender hand, which was scarred with a birthmark that made it look like roast beef, into the crotch of her Lee jeans and stuck a finger into her cooch (Wei Wei's word). At that point, repulsed at the thought of his roast-beef hand, Wei Wei wriggled away from him, found a phone booth, and called her father, who picked her up on the curb outside the mall while Aneesh waited for his mom a hundred feet away, smoking dejectedly next to a trash can. That had happened back in Sulphur, when they were still sophomores at their old high school, before Wei Wei, Janessa, Aneesh, and a few other high achievers got magnetized the hell out of town by this state-funded boarding school two hundred miles north.

"Those boys all have a hard-on the size of Dallas," Wei Wei says, "but a dick the size of…" She lifts her pinkie and wiggles it. "Fuck them. Fuck them," she says to her purple Keds.

Janessa doesn't really have a hunchback, but she does sit hunched and cross-legged on the floor during this revelation, painfully aware of the inescapable twin hazards of her profound sexual inexperience and her even more profound sexual desire—her Scylla and Charybdis: the first an immobile, deadly shoal, the second a whirling vortex.

Okay, she has a little bit of a hunchback. A little scoliosis (*Scylliosis?*). *Un 'tit peu,* as her Cajun Maw-Maw would say. Not enough for a surgically implanted rod to straighten her out—which was the threat from her mother (*Spare the rod, spoil the child!*), and the old-man GP with the shaking hands and cold instruments, if she didn't pull back her shoulders and stand like a lady—but enough to bend her over, bend her sideways, and make her feel like her own spine wants to bend her over and fuck her. (Her younger brother, the juvenile felon, before he got sent away, had taken to calling her Quasimodo. But he was such a terrifying shit in so many ways that the name seemed almost an endearment.) After a long day, it can sometimes feel like she's been carrying around a bucket of lead.

"What's Andrea going to do?" Janessa says, rolling her ailing shoulder up to her ear and back down again. It's already late October, midterm in a semester when GPA matters, and Janessa has two papers to write in two days. She doesn't really have time for this.

Jacqui laughs. It isn't a mean laugh. It isn't even rueful. "Her Maw-Maw is coming to get her. She told her she has a fever." Then she laughs again, brightly, like the joke is on Andrea's Maw-Maw, or on someone, anyway, but not on Andrea.

"We should do something," Janessa says.

"Like what?" Wei Wei says. "Slit Royce's throat?"

"No. Like tell Dr. Ed. Like get him kicked out," Janessa says. "Or public shaming. It's the only way to handle people like that."

"You're an idiot." Wei Wei shucks off her Keds without untying them. She starts picking at the valley between one toe and another. "You ought to wear a bracelet that says *What Would Ayn Rand Do?*"

Janessa hasn't liked Ayn Rand since seventh grade, but Wei Wei won't let it go. So many things about their life in Sulphur, where they were friends desperately since elementary school, Wei Wei will not let go. "I think we should talk to Dr. Ed. I'm not saying tell him what happened. But we should"—under Wei Wei's skeptical gaze, she falters—"express our concerns."

"Oh, just let it be," Jacqui says, as if straight out of her round, soft bosom. "His life will be his punishment." She means Royce. She can love anyone like that, pity anyone. She has had so many families, so many stepsiblings, stepfathers, the most recent of whom touched her in ways no stepfather should. Even still, when she fucks a boy, she says, her favorite part is when he relaxes into her afterward, when he's spent and soft and collapses on her breast like a baby to tend. Where does she get all that love?

Then the suite door hisses, and Andrea asks them why they're all sitting on the floor. She tucks a lank, oily strand of hair behind her ear and steps over Wei Wei's legs, which are stretched across the entryway, then Jacqui's, then Janessa's.

"We're talking about you," Jacqui says.

Andrea's face pinches. She flops her backpack down in the room she shares with Jacqui and stands in the doorway, brittle, pasty, and hesitant. She almost never joins them as a group, but Janessa hears her laughing with Jacqui sometimes beyond their shared wall. Jacqui scoots over and pats the floor. Andrea takes one more look at the three of them. "I'm going to bed," she says, then shuts the door.

The next day Andrea isn't at lunch, and she isn't at dinner, she isn't hiding in the computer lab, and after curfew she is not at her messy desk or in her bed, and no one knows when she will be back, if she ever will.

In World Literature that Friday, Janessa turns in her midterm paper on the Third Day, Tenth Story of the *Decameron,* her favorite, which Dr. Najjar has evaded in class discussions for obvious reasons (*Rustico, what is that thing I see sticking out in front of you, which I do not possess?*) and then sits, as she always does, in front of Norman Sidney Robinson. She likes him. She wishes she could like him more, because he clearly likes her, and if he had the opportunity to lick her neck under the awning of the music building during a rainstorm, he would do it, unlike Adam Braverman, who mashed his lips against hers but would not let her tongue enter the sacred gates of his mouth, and, when the rain slacked off, said he had homework and had to go back to the dorm posthaste. Yes, that's exactly what he said. Sid has a gut and a child beard and sometimes an off-putting odor, but he's smart as hell, and his narrow nose is like an arrow, his blue eyes an enervating poison.

Now, as Dr. Najjar lectures on *The Prince* in her Palestinian purr, her hair flooping over her eyes like a sleeping cat's tail, Sid puts his hands on Janessa's back and begins to rub, starting at the center, where her spine makes its slight digression from rectitude. Then, kneading outward, his sure, curious fingers probe her sides, creep into her armpits, explore the peripheries of her breasts. She leans back and lifts her arms, rests them on her desk. He does this sometimes, and she lets him. She likes it. Why shouldn't she?

This time, though, Dr. Najjar aims a puff of breath at her frizzing bangs and looks pointedly at Janessa. "What do you think it means? When Machiavelli writes, 'The sea is divided; a cloud shows you the road; the rock pours out water; manna rains down; everything unites for your greatness; you ought to do the rest'?"

"A great leader takes advantage of the situation he finds," Janessa says, without missing a beat, "believing, or pretending to believe, that it was made for him." She is surprised herself that some part of her mind has been listening, interested, while another postulates just how wide she would have to spread her legs to accommodate Sid's girth. "Even if his success isn't preordained," she continues, "he should just go ahead and act like it is."

Dr. Najjar nods, kindly but dissatisfied. "And you?" she says to Sid.

Now Janessa knows she has seen. Sid retracts his hands, and Janessa, blushing, turns around, as though attentive for his answer.

"I agree with Janessa," Sid says. *"Carpe diem."*

After waiting, eyes narrowed, for elaboration that never comes, Dr. Najjar moves on. Sid frowns, watches Dr. Najjar intently, and keeps his hands to himself for the rest of class.

Janessa catches up to him in the hallway, and, curling her fingers around his elbow, asks if he's heard about Andrea. He keeps walking but lets her hand stay on his arm and eyes her sidelong, like a mountain might watch a string of climbers making their way antlike to its summit. Andrea Garner, she clarifies.

"Oh, the computer-lab girl. What happened to her?"

"She went home, like maybe for good. Do you know why?"

He breaks away from her hand. "No," he says. His trig class is down a different hall, and these are their crossroads, the spot they always say goodbye. He faces her, watches her down his sharp nose. "Do you?"

Janessa searches her body for pockets in which to hide her hands. "No," she says. She doesn't know him well enough to know whether he's lying.

"That girl's a mess," Sid says. "Do you know what she *does* in the computer lab every night? Let's just say she ain't writing code."

Hasn't Andrea been playing some kind of multi-user game? Not too long ago, she cornered Janessa at the bathroom sink and rattled on about the text-based outer-space world she inhabited as a Jedi knight, and about the Jedi master—in real life, an Ole Miss chem student named Jeff—who had sent her a pair of *Hitchhiker's Guide* socks and now wanted to drive over for a weekend rendezvous. Is that what Sid means? Or, what, was Andrea writing erotica? Getting fingered under the desk? Jerking cocks?

But before Janessa can work it out, Sid, aiming his blue eyes at the bulletin board behind her, asks if she wants to see the foreign film tonight. The poster is a smoky bluish gray and shows a woman with cropped French-girl hair leaning, seated, against a wall. She's in a tiny skirt, sheer black stockings, mile-high heels. She looks like she ought to be smoking a cigarette, but instead, she's gripping a handgun. Janessa says she'll meet him at the theater.

When Aneesh and Johnny Zhao come slinking down the hall, Janessa turns abruptly to go. "She's fucking hot," Johnny says, in his startlingly baritone voice. "I'd let her grip my pistol anytime." Janessa whirls back around, ready to spit, but Johnny is ogling the poster, not her.

Aneesh's eyes are black and startling and apologetic when they land on Janessa and then flick over to Sid. He bumps Johnny with his elbow and says, "Shut the fuck up, dumbass." Not since that long-ago time when they were third-graders together in a gifted special-ed class, crafting pinch pots and annotating *A Wrinkle in Time,* has Aneesh ever spoken other than unkindly to her or about her, if he spoke to her at all, especially after the thing with Wei Wei. But now, it seems, Sid's affection is a shield.

Just outside the main office, Dr. Ed, the frumpish, curly-haired director of the school, stands with his hands resting sort of half on his belly and half on his hips, watching the students go by, like a farmer on his porch, an old man on his fresh-mowed lawn. "Keep the faith, Miss Bourgeois," he says as she passes. He smiles paternally, and she smiles back.

He's a really nice man. He starts to recite "Evangeline," at a volume that's meant neither to be heard nor unheard, like Janessa's father when he sings *"Amor, vida de mi vida,"* à la Plácido Domingo, while he tinkers around in the woodshop, busying his way through her little brother's incarceration.

"This is the forest primeval," says Dr. Ed. "The murmuring pines and the hemlocks, / Bearded with moss, and in garments green . . ." He was an English teacher before being made director. He's easy to talk to, she could talk to him now. But she doesn't. She has to get to class.

After German III and the War in Vietnam, Janessa stops by the mailroom and finds in her box, among a passel of college brochures, a letter from an aunt who lives in Baton Rouge. The aunt, her father's sister, has taken an interest in Janessa, and they write to each other often, typed opuses that fatten envelopes. The aunt has no children. Her letters are as frenetic and sentimental as Janessa's are willfully methodical and stoic. To her aunt, Janessa registers every gripe and outrage, like ninety-five theses, in measured, thesaurus-embellished sentences that quote Hobbes, Camus, Machiavelli. In reply, her aunt quotes God, or what she imagines God might say. But because she's always on Janessa's side, God is on Janessa's side, too, so it's okay.

Back at the dorm, Wei Wei is napping, the covers pulled over her head and her bare feet sticking out the other end. Janessa pries open her aunt's letter, then stretches out on her squeaky twin bed, quiet as she can. With the letter held over her face, she gets flat, pressing the small of her back into the mattress, trying to turn a question mark into an exclamation point.

Wei Wei stirs, rises in a huff, and blunders from the bed toward the foyer, the bathroom.

In this new letter, God is telling Janessa what a bright future she has ahead of her, how she can do anything she dreams of, accomplish anything she puts her mind to, and other such platitudes to which God is prone. *Put your faith in Me, and I will move mountains for you.* Then her aunt goes on to say that she has spoken with Bud Bankston, one of the lawyers at the firm where she is a paralegal, and Bud Bankston has spoken with his buddy in the statehouse, who has spoken with his buddy, a rich man in California, and if Janessa wants, that buddy in California, who also happens to be old pals with the Dean of Admissions at the very university where Janessa and Wei Wei most (desperately! desperately!) want to go, can write a letter on her behalf, make a phone call, push a decision in her favor. He is a really important man. Gives a lot of money to all kinds of things. *Doesn't God work in mysterious ways?* All Janessa has to do is say the word, and it will be so.

Wei Wei returns, pokes around in the minifridge, opens up something that pops and hisses, sits at her desk. Wei Wei does not believe in God. It was one of the first things Janessa learned about her, and in third grade it scared her, but then, Janessa decided she didn't believe in God either, although she is not as ferocious in her unbelief as Wei Wei. She might believe in God, a little.

Wei Wei gets up again, opens the blinds. She clicks on the lamp by Janessa's bed. "How can you read like that?" she says.

"I'm fine," Janessa says. "I can see."

"I know. Because I turned on a light."

They may as well be sisters, the way they treat each other. They fight like that. They love each other like that. Don't they? Their families treat each other like family, too. Or rather, Wei Wei's family treats Janessa's family like family. When the Chens found out Janessa's father had cashed out his retirement to pay for her brother's legal expenses and supposed rehabilitation (an insulting surprise to everyone when *that* bill came), Wei Wei and her mother, Miss Eunice, in her grand straw hat, bustled into the kitchen one day with groceries—boxes and boxes of groceries—from the Chen family store. Whole milk and American cheese and Chinese cabbage. So many nonperishables it looked like they had raided the church donation box at Thanksgiving. Janessa's mother was so grateful she wept. It was ridiculous how she wept, how she threw herself upon Eunice. "We sure do thank you. We thank you so much for your kindness." They weren't even remotely starving. Wei Wei, with irritating tenderness, said to Janessa's mother, "It's nothing, Miss Pam. Mommy wanted to do it." Janessa's father was out back, turning bowls or pens or dildos or bludgeons, who knows, on the lathe, with the record player up loud. When the Chens left, Janessa's mother made her swear not to tell him where the food had come from. It was one thing to have Chinese friends. It was another when the Chinese friends thought they were better than you. Her mother didn't say it that way, but Janessa knew. That's how her father thought.

Now she and Wei Wei have applied to the same colleges, including and especially the one in California with its walls like warm beach sands, its broad plazas and offbeat essay questions. They have watched the promotional VHS many times. Why this college above all others, above even Harvard and Yale and Princeton, upon which so many of their classmates have set their sights? They could argue the point extensively and rationally, but in truth it's more of a feeling, a tingle in their bones. The college promotional video has entered their VHS rotation with *Vertigo* (for its tantalizing shots of San Francisco), U2's *Rattle and Hum,* and *The Persecution and Assassination of Jean-Paul Marat as Performed by the Inmates of the Asylum of Charenton Under the Direction of the Marquis de Sade* (which Janessa recorded from a 4 a.m. airing on AMC). Why the obsession with any of those things, really? You can't argue a tingle.

As Janessa ventures deeper into the aunt's letter, forgetting her crooked, aching spine, Wei Wei flumps onto her own bed. Now the aunt is describing a visit with Janessa's brother at the new juvenile detention center, which she says is much nicer than the old one. Clean. Less echoey. The lawyers are working on getting him out early, because why should he have so much of his life ruined for fifteen minutes of bad behavior? He's just a boy.

He is two years younger than Janessa, but she is more afraid of her brother than of anyone else. When he was eight, he took her parakeet out of its cage and squeezed it until it was dead, and everyone said it was an accident, but Janessa saw the look in his eyes when he decided to do it. Five years later, he broke into the neighbors' house and set fire to the mother's cancer wig while the grandfather slept down the hall. He only got probation for that. Within the year, though, he entered another neighbor's house and tried to set another fire, this time to the actual hair of a twelve-year-old girl. They were just playing around, he said. The girl, whose mother discovered her tied with a feather boa to the footboard of her bed, her hair singed almost to the scalp, declined to corroborate his story, however. For that one he went to kid jail, but along the way there had been other stuff besides the parakeet and the fires. "Accidents." Including one involving Wei Wei and a hot curling iron. Now the state makes Janessa's parents pay for his caging. When her father brought the first bill down to the Office of Juvenile Justice, thinking it was some kind of mistake, they told him it was in fact no mistake. "Think of it as child support," the social worker said. "You believe in child support, don't you?" Happily, Janessa's boarding school is all but free. So, hey, at least they're coming out even.

Somewhere down the hallway of Third East, a roving band of girls makes a cheerful ruckus. Doors slam shut.

Wei Wei slurps her soda and says, philosophically, "You never ask how I'm doing."

"What?"

"It's like you don't even care. You just come in here, lay down on your bed, and you don't even say hello."

"You were sleeping."

"Even when I'm not sleeping."

"Fine." Janessa raises herself onto her elbows, her spine whining like a rusted hinge, and turns her neck, in pain, to look at Wei Wei. "How are you doing?"

"Don't ask because I told you to ask. Ask because you care."

Janessa's back hurts, her brother is a psychopath, and her

family is broke, thanks to her brother. Wei Wei is right: she doesn't care. To care would be to drown in caring. Still, for heaven's sake. "Wei Wei, I care. Obviously I care."

"Not obviously. But whatever. It's just who you are. I'll either learn to accept it or I won't."

"Okay." Janessa folds her aunt's letter violently and stuffs it back in its envelope. "Let me know what you decide."

She shoves her body up and out of bed, stalks out of the suite. The hall is empty, fluorescent. The lounge is empty, fluorescent. The TV, muted, plays an episode of *The Simpsons.* On the three flights of stairs leading down to the lobby, her bare feet slap the steps. Where the hell is she going shoeless? She reaches the bottom of the steps and turns around, heads back up.

Wei Wei hasn't moved. She's sitting in bed, waiting or fuming.

"What's wrong?" Janessa says. Her throat is so full of caring she's choking on it.

"Nothing's wrong," Wei Wei says. "I'm fine. It's just the principle of it."

Wei Wei is clearly not fine. Her eyes are all puffed up. Her face is red.

Then Jacqui bursts into the foyer sing-yelling, "Who wants some gas-station greasies?" and Wei Wei, thank the God she doesn't believe in, leaps up and calls, "I do!"

She and Jacqui go into Jacqui's room, where Andrea's side is still as disorderly as the day she left. A fanned-out heap of sci-fi novels on her desk. Dirty undies, crusty side up, kicked halfway under her bed. A poster of Sigourney Weaver gaping awestruck through the glass of a space helmet. Wei

Wei and Jacqui slam shut the door and crank up the P. J. Harvey. Janessa can hear them shouting along: "You snake, you crawled between my legs. Said want it all it's yours you bet."

Sid is waiting outside the college cinema, but not just Sid. It's all of them: Aneesh, Johnny Zhao, a sulky girl from New Orleans named Autumn who has lately started linking fingers with Aneesh in public. And Royce Bright. Something in Janessa's chest wobbles when she sees him, like a finger poking her sternum from the inside. *Fucking rapist,* she thinks. He's taller than the others, pale, his arms too long for his long body. They are huddled together, all of them smoking except Sid, who rises up on his toes when he sees Janessa but does not smile or welcome her. He turns and opens the door, goes through it first, gives it an extra push so it won't shut in her face.

Sid leads the way to a row of seats in the dead middle of the theater, and though Aneesh has the sense to hang back, Johnny does not, and so Johnny sits next to Sid, Janessa sits next to Johnny, and then Royce slides in next to Janessa. Aneesh and Autumn take the end of the row, where they will spend most of the movie groping each other, a single dark shadow. Janessa cranes her neck over Johnny's shaggy black head to make eye contact with Sid, but he won't look at her. Royce props the balls of his feet on the seat in front of him and angles his legs into a tent. When his elbow bumps Janessa's on the armrest, he apologizes indifferently but politely, withdraws his arm. What's especially fucked up is that he smells good. Not cologne-and-aftershave good, just person-good. He smells intensely like someone she knows, the gentle spice of warm hair and worn clothes. Janessa tucks her arms into her sides, folds her hands in her lap, leans toward Johnny, who keeps making a grating noise in his throat, as regular as a dripping faucet.

Royce turns, regards her sleepily. "So what's new in the whiskey business?" he says. Janessa fixes her eyes on the velvet curtain.

The lights go down. Janessa shifts onto one hip, crosses her bare legs away from Royce, and tugs at her miniskirt, which she now feels like a moron for wearing. The film begins, the flapping of the projector audible for a moment alongside Johnny's rhythmic throat-clearing, before the music pipes in, and on screen, wet pavement scrolling fast. Four punks charge forth, on a mission. They break into a pharmacy. One of the punks is a woman, and she's looking at another of the punks, the handsomest one, lustfully, her mouth slack, transfixed. "I need it," she says, in French, as translated by the subtitles, and she might mean drugs or she might mean cock, but for the next five minutes of guns and smoke and idiots shouting, the ladypunk props herself listlessly under a table, wearing headphones. When a freaked-out cop with eyes like Dr. Ed's finds her there—the cop's face so open, so intimately visible—she presses a pistol to his neck and fires.

Out of the darkness next to Janessa, Johnny says, in his absurdly deep voice, "Oh shit."

The woman gets a life sentence and loses it completely in the courtroom. "Motherfuckers! Motherfuckers!" Headbutts, roundhouse kicks. In an industrial basement, tied to a chair, she thinks she's being executed (did the dumbass not even listen to her sentence?) and starts crying for her mother. "Mama! Mama!"

Janessa's throat tightens. Her eyes water. *Fucking psychopath. She deserves whatever she gets.* Royce's arm has again claimed the armrest. The warmth of his bare elbow repels Janessa's bare elbow like a flame.

The ladypunk gets sent to a finishing school for sexy ninja assassins: computers, weapons, martial arts, social graces. She meets a very nice grocery boy. "I want you," she says to the grocery boy, getting on top of him. The grocery boy says, "Don't start what you can't stop." She falls in love, finds her humanity, whatever. Janessa liked her better as a psychopath.

When the credits roll and the lights come up, Janessa turns to Johnny and says, "What a crock of shit."

Johnny looks at her like he's never seen her before in his life.

Outside, they gather around Aneesh's cigarette lighter as though it will save their lives in a blizzard. Janessa makes it about twenty feet down the sidewalk when she feels a hand on her shoulder.

"Come wander around with us," Sid says.

"Wander where?"

Sid shrugs his whole body. "Let's go check out the fountain. Some jackass put dish soap in it again."

On hot nights—there are still some, even in October—Janessa, Wei Wei, and Jacqui (never Andrea, who was always in the computer lab) visit the fountain, climb the brick pyramid to the top, in their clothes, and take turns sitting on the gushing stream. It isn't lost on them that it feels fucking good. They make jokes about "Dr. Wang"

(Wei Wei started that). But it's also magical not in a clit-centered way. They play in the fountain, too. Three Graces, three mermaids, three fairies—like she used to play when she was five—only fucking a fountain. *A liminal space,* that's what Dr. Najjar would call it. When this year is over, she will miss this fountain, this nighttime wandering, but not all that damned much. The university in California, too, has fountains—featured on the VHS!—and nighttime.

Tonight, the fuckable fairy fountain is spewing white suds, just as Sid predicted. Like the lacy train of a wedding gown, the suds trail down the bricks and puddle at the base. Lights around the fountain turn purple then gold then purple then gold, the university colors. Janessa and Sid sit together on the ground, against a low brick rim. Aneesh, Autumn, Royce, and Johnny move to the far side, and though their laughter sometimes sails over the gush of water like spitballs lobbed at a blackboard, Janessa and Sid might as well be alone.

Sid's face goes purple gold purple gold. A meaty hand rests on his knee, the leather band of a watch digging into his wrist. The hand finds her nape, squeezes, rubs. She leans her back into him and he draws her in with his arm, pulls her head close, buries his nose in her hair. He strokes her arm with his fingertips, finds her hand, covers it with his. She leans in closer, deeper, and he is all around her, legs and arms, his hands crawling up her shirt. He pinches a nipple and she pushes her shoulders back into his chest, the wide, soft, solid wall of him. His nose presses into her ear, his tongue finds her neck. What can only be his cock (*Rustico, what is that thing?*) pokes at her lower back. He shifts his weight, emits a low, breathy groan, and up from the warmth of his great bulk wafts an odor, not quite cheese. Sid flinches.

"Actually, that's annoying right now," she says, and shrugs away from him.

"Sorry."

"My back," she says. He knows about the scoliosis. It isn't that, but she feels bad. For him and for herself. She sits up straight, rolls her shoulders, flops her neck from side to side. Casually she says, "What's happening with you, college-wise?"

Sid hisses through his teeth. "Do we have to talk about that?"

"Where are you applying?"

"LSU. LSU-E. LSU-X, -Y, and -Z."

"Not good enough," she says. "You should be applying to Harvard or whatever."

Sid is the math star, the history star, the chemistry and biology star. Plus, his family lives in a shithole in Vinton and his mother is a hoarder: books, cowboy boots, live animals, you name it. Janessa and Wei Wei dropped him off there once, on a weekend trip home, and you couldn't even see the living-room floor.

"Just tell them how poor you are," she says. "They eat that shit up." That's what she's hoping for herself, anyway. The psychopath brother who brings the already-poor family to actual ruin.

"Please." He hefts himself up.

Johnny and Royce have come around to their side of the fountain, leaving Aneesh and Autumn to do whatever they're doing over there, and when Johnny makes a general announcement that he has to take a piss, Sid departs with him.

Royce sidles over to Janessa and lowers himself down, like they're old friends, do this all the time. He reaches into the fountain, scoops up a handful of foam, holds it to his mouth and blows it away like dandelion fluff. He says, laconically, "That movie really pissed you off, huh? I get it." His voice thrums. "If I were a woman, it would piss me off too. Put on your lipstick, learn to smile, serve the state. I totally get it. You're a feminist."

"No, I'm not."

"Oh, okay." He roots around in his pants pockets and pulls out a plastic baggie, a tiny glass pipe. He takes a pinch from the baggie and nudges it into the bowl with his fingertip, then rolls up the baggie and stuffs it back into his pants. He looks at her, takes her in. "I'm a feminist," he says.

Janessa burps out a laugh.

"What? I'm not afraid to say it. Why are you?"

"I'm not afraid."

She thinks of the parakeet, broken in her brother's hand, its head dangling off his palm. When her brother smiled at her, offering the bird like a handful of candy, that's when she was afraid. Of this motherfucker, she is not afraid. She is not afraid! Had Andrea been afraid? Is that why whatever happened to her happened to her?

"I'm not afraid," she says again. "To say I'm a feminist would be to admit exclusion from traditional forms of power. And to admit exclusion would only validate that power. Fuck you. I'm just as powerful as you are. I don't need feminism to tell me that. Fuck you." Spittle flies onto her shoes.

Royce laughs and offers her the pipe, a lighter. "Ladies first."

"I don't want that."

107

Now Sid and Johnny are back. Sid thinks Royce has been moving in on his territory, Janessa can tell. He won't look at her, won't look at Royce; he bounces his weight like a boxer gearing up. He wants to hurt somebody but won't. Royce holds out the pipe to Sid, who takes it, tokes, blows a furious plume of smoke that glows gold, then purple, then gold.

Janessa's spine is murderous. She'll be damned if she'll lie supine before these assholes, but the pinch that started in her neck is now skittering up and down her naked legs like a rat trapped in a wall. She needs to lie flat. Holding on to the ledge of the fountain, she lowers herself to the brick path, yanks down the ever-crawling hem of her skirt.

The scheming stars gather in conspiratorial patterns: Orion's nebulous dick and his bright belt of skulls with their biblically ladylike names—Alnilam, Alnitak, Mintaka—and Bellatrix the Warrioress tucked up into his armpit. Janessa had a constellation phase around the same time as the Ayn Rand phase. She remembers them all, can spot them all. Orion should be shot out of the sky. *Fucking rapist.*

Royce's face intrudes upon the mighty hunter's crotch. "What is she doing?"

"Fuck if I know," Sid says.

"Janessa?" It's Wei Wei, suddenly nearby for some reason, shouting. Rapid footsteps on the bricks, then Wei Wei crouching down, close to her face. "What the fuck?" She twists her neck up to Royce and Sid. "Why is she on the ground?"

They don't even offer a shrug or an eye roll, just slip away, out of Janessa's field of vision.

Wei Wei asks her where the hell she's been.

They fight the whole way home, Janessa's rage rising in a low, guttering arc like a distress flare. "I don't need another mother," she says, venomous.

"What were you doing with those guys? You didn't even tell us you were going out."

"Why do you need to know?"

"It's just considerate."

"Maybe I don't want to be considerate," Janessa says, and then something else she's been thinking lately: "Maybe we shouldn't go to the same college. Or if we do, we should have different friends."

Wei Wei practically skids to a stop, then she trots to catch up and says, breathless, "Your brother burned me with a curling iron." Janessa charges on. "And you told me not to tell. Remember? You told me not to tell, and I didn't. Now you need new friends? What in the fuck is wrong with you?"

Janessa huffs up the low hill to Caddo, Wei Wei trailing. The half-lidded windows of the dorm regard her, their scrubby, battered blinds pulled to cockeyed angles, and behind them so many girls—all those girls in cockeyed states of undress and desire.

On Janessa's bed lie a clutch of phone messages, two from her aunt, another from her father. She already knows why her father is calling. He has asked her to write something sisterly and persuasive on her brother's behalf, something to show the court, to have on record, for whatever good it will do. She alone in the family has this power. Her subjects and verbs agree. Her sentences are complex and compound. They need something in writing for a hearing next week, but she has not even started, can think of little to say in her brother's defense beyond an abstract plea for the kind of mercy due to all human beings, and she isn't sure she can argue persuasively even for that. Flay him alive, she wants to say. Bind his ass to a Judas cradle and let him scream. But then she remembers his warm little three-year-old body snug against hers for Saturday morning cartoons, his dreamy, petroleum-black eyes and maple-syrup breath. Nessa! Nessa! Did she only imagine that boy?

On the pay phone that serves the whole of Third East, Janessa reaches her aunt, who is working late on a corporate case. She's doing most of the heavy lifting for her boss, a lawyer, who—she explains, with cheerful castigation—has flown his new (fourth) wife to a sunny beach in Florida for the weekend (like, flown her himself, in his Cessna) and left Janessa's aunt to finish an appellate brief that has to be filed first thing Monday morning, but *That's all right, it's ALL right,* she knows what she's doing, has done it hundreds of times in the twenty years she's worked for this guy, ought to be a lawyer herself by now, but God has a different plan for her. Janessa's aunt is just as daffy on the phone as she is on the page, but one gets caught up in it, like syrup in a cotton-candy spinner.

"Listen," her aunt says, "I want to put you on the phone with Bud Bankston, the one I was telling you about in my letter. Did you get my letter? Hold on and I'll transfer you over."

Janessa says she doesn't want to talk to Bud Bankston.

"I know you don't want to talk to him, but, sweet love, you *ought* to talk to him. He knows all about you. How good you did on your tests. How smart you are. He really wants to help you." Her aunt starts telling her what sounds like a joke, about a good Christian man who refuses to be rescued in a flood, tells everyone who tries, *God will save me! Go rescue someone else!* And when he drowns and goes to heaven and accuses God of forsaking him in his hour of need, God says, *You idiot, I sent a car, a canoe, and a helicopter. What more did you want?* "Janessa, let God do His work for you," her aunt says. "Accept help when it's offered."

"I don't want that kind of help," Janessa says.

By Monday morning, when Andrea is still not back, Janessa tells Wei Wei and Jacqui that she's going to talk to Dr. Ed.

"Don't," Wei Wei says. "What's the point?"

"It's not yours to tell," Jacqui says.

No one has heard from Andrea, but none of them expected to. Even when she was here, in the same room, she was so deep within herself that she might as well have been a pile of laundry. They had lived together their entire junior year, and what did they know about her? That she had grown up in Lafayette and worked at Popeyes during the summers. That she was a slob among many teenage slobs. That her toothbrush was always purple and her toothpaste always uncapped. That phone calls, when she got them, were from her grandmother or, for a brief time, from Jeff the Jedi master. That she lived with her grandparents but not why. That she preferred history to chemistry, trig to English, Doc Martens to Keds, reptiles to mammals, *Heathers* to *The Princess Bride,* and the company of green text on a black screen to that of her flesh-and-blood suitemates. When they all shared secrets, Andrea did not share secrets. She may very well have had secrets, and had she shared them, they would not be Janessa's to tell, it's true. But this one? This one belongs to all of them.

"It's a public-health issue," Janessa says. "Do you want that guy roaming around campus?"

"Royce Bright is not going to rape you," Jacqui says. "I'm guessing he's all raped out."

"I'm not afraid of that. But he can't just go around like God will always part the sea for him."

"What do you expect Dr. Ed to do about it?" Wei Wei says. "And that's even if he believes you, which he probably will, because he likes you, and he's a nice guy—but then what? You can't prove it."

"It isn't yours to tell," Jacqui repeats.

Nevertheless.

When she tries to see Dr. Ed, his office is crowded with men in suits, or only three men in suits, actually, in the way that three men in suits can seem like twenty. Janessa recognizes one of the men, from drop-offs and pickups, as Royce's father, Royce Bright the Elder. The men in suits seem to have just arrived, are making their introductions, shaking hands with Dr. Ed, and when they move into the office, out of the doorway, there is Royce himself, slouched in the scolding chair. Sid, too, in the other scolding chair. He sees her and averts his eyes. Dr. Ed closes the door.

By afternoon, everyone knows all about it: Royce Bright and Norman Sidney Robinson have been expelled, apparently for smoking pot. Or for possessing pot and the instruments by which one might smoke it. So long, boys. We've got what's called *zero tolerance* on this campus.

"You see?" Jacqui says. "Justice is served."

Janessa feels bad about Sid, who is not, after all, such an irremediable asshole, and it wasn't even his stuff anyway. Still, yes. Maybe it isn't justice exactly, but problem solved. The truth will out, albeit a watered-down version of it, oblique but actionable.

A quiet week passes. During this quiet week, Janessa composes a set of essays to send to the university where she most wants to go, including one in which she works the destitute family, psychopathic brother, and scoliosis into an elaborate metaphor involving kitchen appliances and perishables that are a single day past expiration. Don't ask how she does it. It's a wonder to behold. She even manages some sympathy for her brother. The sympathy is mostly self-serving, to impress the admissions people. Still, she can adapt that bit into a letter to send to her father for the court. Two birds, one stone. She trades essays with Wei Wei, who it turns out has written her own elaborate metaphor about kitchen appliances and perishable food—Miss Eunice the tie that binds, apparently—and they are each a little bit misty and reverent reading these essays, as if lighting votives at the altar of their friendship.

When Miss Eunice asks to speak to Janessa on the hallway phone and invites her to come along in the spring for a visit to the longed-for college, all expenses paid, Janessa doesn't refuse outright. Instead, she says she'll think about it, and she does. Miss Eunice wants the girls to stay together, to look after each other, always. Maybe that's even possible. Maybe Janessa even wants that. *Accept help when it's offered. Carpe diem. Etcetera, etcetera.*

By the end of the quiet week, she and Wei Wei are watching *The Fugitive* together again, reenacting scenes from *The Persecution and Assassination of Jean-Paul Marat as Performed by the Inmates of the Asylum of Charenton Under the Direction of the Marquis de Sade,* with Wei Wei as Marat, in the laundry basket/bathtub, and Janessa as Sade, slinking along the walls like a nervous rat. "Nature herself would watch unmoved if we destroyed the entire human race. I hate Nature." (That's Janessa's favorite part.) They jump on their twin beds, singing about tumbrel drivers and the gangrenous dead.

When Jacqui enters the suite, she says, "Girls, girls, what am I going to do with you?" and when the sun goes down, they all go off to the fountain, to pay a visit to Dr. Wang.

At breakfast the following Monday, Janessa scans the cafeteria for the right hair: Wei Wei's choppy self-cut bob and Jacqui's mocha 'fro. Wei Wei and Jacqui, already seated, are craning their necks all around, looking for someone, but not, apparently, for Janessa, whom they greet not at all when she tugs a chair out with her foot and plops her tray on the table.

Then Wei Wei, finding their target, bumps Jacqui with an elbow, gestures with her chin. Janessa sits down. "He's back," Wei Wei says.

At a table near the silent jukebox, Royce Bright sits with his cheek propped serenely on one hand. He smiles and bobs his head and twirls his fork around his plate, listening to Johnny Zhao while Aneesh tries to wave down Autumn, who has told Jacqui that Royce's father called in a favor from the state senator responsible for the school's funding bills. The stipulation is that Royce won't be allowed to live on campus.

114

"He gets a house instead," Wei Wei says. "One of those big ones on the river."

"What about Sid?" Janessa asks.

Jacqui unwraps one tiny butter packet and then another, plopping them both into a bowl of undercooked grits. She stirs the butter, tastes the grits, makes a face, and shoves the bowl into a half-full cup of Coke that wobbles and nearly topples, and when rather than toppling it comes to rest, Jacqui pushes it over with dispassionate precision. "I'm done with this shit," she says. Coke pools on the table. The cup clatters onto the floor and rolls.

Dr. Ed, with his soft paunch and gentle curls, opens his office door when Jacqui taps it, as though he's been waiting just on the other side for exactly this tap. He welcomes the three girls in, gracious, affecting un-surprise. They sit in the scolding chairs, and they tell him everything they know about Andrea and Royce, which isn't much but is from Andrea herself.

Dr. Ed closes his eyes, pinches the bridge of his nose.

"So why is he back here?" Jacqui asks. She practically glows with fury.

Dr. Ed hides his face in his hands, and the girls consider in silence the bald patch at the top of his scalp, the curls that do not quite conceal it.

He says, finally looking up at them again, "You girls are brave. You're very brave."

Are they? Janessa thought this would feel like vengeance, release. It feels like nothing. Like a bald patch at the top of a kind man's head. Like some quiet violence they've done to this kind man.

He does not tell them what they already know—that Royce's deliverance has been bought—he just apologizes, again and again, until they can't bear his suffering anymore, and they leave, unsure what, if anything, they've accomplished.

They wait for something to happen. But days later, Royce is still passing them in the halls, still sitting in their classes, still colonizing their small world with his lazy authority. Meanwhile, Andrea has not come back and neither has Sid. Jacqui wants to call Andrea, but none of them have her number and the RAs won't give it out.

Then, on the Monday before Thanksgiving, the whole school is called in for an assembly. The students gather in the auditorium, and the mood is festive, because last time they were called suddenly to assemble, it was for an impromptu cookout and a surprise performance by a visiting troupe of child actors hilariously misquoting Shakespeare. Janessa, Wei Wei, and Jacqui sit together at the back, where they always sit. When Dr. Ed crosses the stage to the podium and taps the microphone, the auditorium goes gradually quiet. No one dims the house lights. No one opens the curtain behind him.

This is it, thinks Janessa. *Something is going to happen.* They've been waiting for this, whatever it is, to happen.

"Students," Dr. Ed says. His amplified sigh gusts to the room's far corners. He stares at the microphone, closes his eyes. His gentleness is galling. Janessa wants to grab his curls and slam his face against the podium to get him to say whatever he's going to say. After what seems an eternity, he tells them, as though reading from an index card, that someone has passed away.

When he says Andrea's name, Jacqui sucks in air. Janessa's vision frays at the edges. She can't make her teeth unclench. Wei Wei presses her nails into Janessa's wrist. Dr. Ed is still talking, and the news is air whooshing past, through Janessa's chest, up her spine, out with her breath. It feels like a great walloping nothing. Andrea's things are still in her room. Her undies are still on the floor. Her toothpaste is still uncapped.

It's okay, Dr. Ed tells them, to feel whatever they may be feeling. A suicide leaves so many unanswered questions. He goes on for an unbearably long time, speaking in platitudes while Janessa waits for him to say the one thing that matters, and when abruptly he's done, without saying that thing, he leaves the stage and no one rises and no one speaks. Finally, a few students stand, wait for others in the row to stand. They advance down the aisles like a communion line.

Royce sits in the way back of the auditorium, nearest the exit, his long body angled on an elbow, his long legs crossed and stretched out into the aisle. He watches the procession at his leisure. His sleepy eyes find Janessa. He waves a little wave. *So what's new in the whiskey business?*

In another week, Dr. Ed steps down of his own accord, at least as reported publicly, and goes back to his Longfellow and his Shakespeare. The man who takes his place cannot quote at length from *Evangeline,* but he sure as hell knows how to shake hands and with whom. Royce Bright stays in his house on the lake and graduates with the rest of them.

He is admitted to a good-enough college, after which he will no doubt attend a good-enough law school, become a prosecutor and then a judge, and—who knows?—maybe even end up on the Supreme Court one day. Stranger things have happened.

Sid sends a single letter to Janessa in which he writes about the half-mummified cat that he found curled up under the piles of books and boots on his mother's bedroom floor and also apologizes for that night at the fountain when he really wanted to call her a cock-teasing little cunt but didn't and is glad he didn't, because now maybe they can still be friends. Can't they still be friends? Janessa's brother, meanwhile, assaults another kid so brutally and unaccidentally in juvenile detention that even her beautiful letter with its counterfeit sympathy cannot rescue him from his inevitable transfer to a federal pen.

Miss Eunice continues to help Janessa's parents with groceries. For years. And Janessa, too, learns to accept help when it's offered. She talks to her aunt who talks to Bud Bankston who talks to his buddy who talks to *his* buddy who talks to the Dean of Admissions, and Lord in heaven, does it not feel like manna raining down, like water from a rock, when Janessa gets into the coveted university with a hefty scholarship. Wei Wei does not get in (don't worry about Wei Wei, though, she gets a full ride to University of Chicago), and Janessa never stops worrying over what's to become of her spine.

So, in other words, nothing's new. There's nothing new in the whiskey business.

When Pluto Lost
His Planetary Status

This is my dad's favorite joke:

There was this old boy in the nuthouse who used to sit in his room scribbling. He scribbled all day long and most of the night, and never said a word for twenty-five years. The doctors kept watch on him, tried to figure out what he was drawing, but couldn't make out a thing. Those twenty-five years went by, and one day out of the blue, he wanted to talk to his doctor. Sitting there in that doctor's office, the old boy was jittery, excited. He spread his mess of drawings out on the doctor's desk.

For the first time in twenty-five years, he opened his mouth and said, "Doctor, I've finally done it. All these years I've been working, and I've finally done it. I've designed a mechanical clock that will keep time so accurately that in 20 million years, it will have lost only a quarter of a second. By God, I've done it!"

The doctor just looked the old boy up and down, then looked at the papers. He flipped through the drawings, turning them upside down and right-side up again. He stacked them into a neat pile and tapped the edges on the desk. Then the doctor handed the papers back to the old boy. "That's all well and good, but really," the doctor said, "who gives a shit?"

In 1905, the search began. They followed Gemini across the sky, taking picture after picture. They traced and measured every movement. With telescopes, photographic plates, blink microscopes, patience, one day they would catch him as he fled fast into darkness among the stationary stars. He was tugging on Neptune and Uranus, bending their orbits. He must be larger than Jupiter. He could not escape.

I'm about to blow the big secret about you. If you think you can't handle it, you especially better read on. Brace yourself. The big secret is this. (Brace yourself now.)

Every story you know about your father, or your sister, or your closest friends, I've got one to match it (well, yes, of course, you say—but no, *listen*)—legends, your family mythology: the time your grandfather caught your mom, as a child, running through the house and, as punishment, made her run laps around the yard in the heat of the afternoon until she fainted; or the time your uncle dove into his above-ground pool, busted the siding, and the gushing flood set loose toward the house, with your aunt at the door leaning forward, hands out like a football player, as though she could block the onslaught of water—heroes with formidable hubris, submitting to divine and poetic justice—I know just as many. Every kind of love you have felt, for every irreplaceable person, I have felt love just as profound and worshipful and inimitable and hopelessly banal.

The biggest secret, though, is that everyone else already knows this secret about you; but so trivial is your triviality that no one (but me) bothers to speak of it. (It could be, yes it could be, that I only want you stripped of myth.) And you at least have the comfort of knowing this about me.

Here's my own myth of origins:

From nowhere and nothing, I was vomited into light and color.

A bayou. A wharf. Sundown. The erotic smell of barbecue, wild onion, water, sweat, rot. Time eating his children. My dad eating a leg, then a breast. A crowd of family lines up at the pit on the wharf, my (half) sister in the rear. I don't know the boy in front of her. I'd like some chicken too. The boy looks back at me. Looks back at me. Grins. I don't know him. I feel embarrassed, regurgitated. I only want some chicken. My (half) sister turns around, and I recognize her and her face and eyes and cheeks.

She says, *This is your brother, Dad doesn't know, and don't tell him.*

The boy looks at me. He's nearly grown. He grins. I recognize him, his face and cheeks, and the way his eyes apologize for his body, for his breathing, for his eyes apologizing. Another bastard, like me and like her. We're a long line of bastards, and we're waiting for chicken. Our dad yells for more chicken. We move slowly up the line. Our dad yells for another beer. Some bastard gets him one.

In 1930, they finally found him, sneaking around Delta Geminorum. They charted and named him, estimated his orbit and his diameter. They discovered too late that the celestial object they named Pluto was much smaller than expected; arguably, too small to be a planet, and too surrounded by other objects exactly or somewhat like him. This impostor showed himself, claimed the name, but he is not the one they sought. Or perhaps he is, and he only defies their expectations.

His status as planet may yet be revoked. They may strip him of his godhood. He will no longer be the ninth and farthest.

There was once a man who, because of certain obsessive and delusional qualities (he kept himself awake for maddening days at a time measuring oscillations and perfecting escapements), committed himself to an insane asylum. The man never spoke a word. Medicated and undisturbed, he kept to the asylum's prescribed schedule but spent hours alone every day scribbling figures and drafting blueprints in his room. Reams of indecipherable drawings had to be cleared weekly by nurses. Still more remained neatly filed in his desk. Since the man seemed to be causing no harm to himself or anyone else, the doctors allowed this to continue and supplied him with as much paper as he needed. Finally, after twenty-five years of scribbling and silence, the man spoke.

"I'm done," he said to his doctor. He spread his drawings out on the desk, gestured for the doctor to have a look. "I can be in the world again."

The doctor bent over the precise, immaculate circles and lines, the pages and pages of graphs and elaborate equations, gears, arcs, numbers calculated to seemingly infinite decimal places. The doctor was confounded. "What exactly is it you've been drawing all these years?"

"I have perfected a mechanical clock," the man said, "which, under ideal conditions, will keep time so accurately that in 20 million years, it will have lost only a quarter of a second!"

The doctor took a step back and looked at the man. The man's eyes never met the doctor's, never settled. He was admiring every detail of his own work. His hands trembled, longing to trace and retrace the lines. The skin on his face was thin and wrinkled. His hair and beard had gone white.

"That's all well and good," the doctor said. "But really, old man, who gives a shit?"

If you were on the page exactly as you are in life, and my drawing of you were no more evocative than a snapshot, at least I would have had the pleasure of tracing every shadow and line of you, as I cannot in life.

The pencil is my fingertip, exploring you. I acquaint myself with the tiniest curve of your eyelashes and the marbled gloss of your eyes, the particular light of this moment reflected in your eyes. I shade gently the whiteness that will be your bicep—the smooth, hairless flash of skin when you fold your arms behind your head, and your T-shirt sleeve slips back toward your shoulder, showing more and more arm, until I can see, against delicate pale, the brown hairs of your underarm. I'll draw them too. It's the most naked I've seen you, and proves that you are touchable, and if I were able to touch you, I would feel softness; and if I were able to smell you—if I were able to touch and smell you—I would not have to draw you.

As you lie in the grass, the sun, dappled through oak leaves and summer clouds, lights your body in a way that it never will again. Your body will change or die. The clouds will disintegrate, reform as entirely new clouds. The sun, the earth, and the gasses of the earth have been whirling through all Space and Time only for the purpose of finally lighting your body at this moment. Humans have been breeding and dying, and breeding and dying so that now, finally, you could lie there in the grass lighted in this way, and I could sit here cross-legged, recording the light.

He had been part of the coup to oust his own father, and with his brothers, he divided our world: sky, water, death. Of these, his part was death. Father gone, Time defeated, he still longed to be chewed up, swallowed, and disgorged. He had come to expect an existence divided—portions of life doled out as rations, small, edible, and inhabitable. There would be now only vastness and immortality. So he chose a realm of perpetual endings, that he might at least have some reminder what it meant to have endings and beginnings. He tapped the earth with his trident, and the earth opened up. He descended, and thereafter stayed hidden below, an observer of those who could finish in one world and begin in another.

We move up and up the line, the crowd around us thinning, until we reach the pit, and our dad beside it amid bones and cans, tossing more bones and cans off the wharf into the bayou. I have been bragging, quietly, to everyone—*this is my brother, this is my brother, this is my brother.* I have no reason to love him, but I do. Our bodies resonate. We share an orbit.

Our dad looks us up and down—me, my sister, my brother. He is trembling too; his body knows. He chews his chicken. My sister and I drop our eyes, ashamed, and prepare to be eaten. My brother steps forward. He has yet to learn. He says to our dad, *Yes, it's true. And you know it. Look at yourself. Look at me. Look at her, and her.* I watch our dad turn red, eyes bulging, as though once again a woman, or the world, or some too-just god has tied him up and set him aflame with his own matches and kerosene. Used his own damned matches against him.

He says, *I got no kids.*

My brother says, *Yes. You do.*

Our dad lunges at him, but staggers, loses balance, tumbles with his lawn chair into the bayou. I tell my brother he should have expected it, as we had learned to expect it—*it* being what you deserve *and* what you don't deserve, with no particular distinction between the two.

He believed in the clock and its pieces: lantern pinions, sprocket arbors, wheels, balance, and random walk. He believed in the verge escapement, as though it were, yes, the mechanism behind the pendulum, but also a brink he himself might jump from, to fall endlessly under a force not his own. He believed that the words and pieces were more than words and pieces, and that if he measured, put them together precisely, he could find Time (as it had hidden in the old men's pockets—silver or gold, engraved, on chains—when, as a boy, he would wander the square, under a clock tower that always read four hours fast, saying, *Hey mister, do you have the right time? Excuse me, sir, do you . . . ?*).

He jumped from the brink. He fell.

On paper, the pieces merged, drawn to scale, until they could be, for all their detail, a working machine. The gears ticked off seconds and portions of seconds; the pendulums swung in gentle arcs; he felt Time moving beneath his pencil and the pulse of it traveling up his hands, through his body.

Meanwhile, he grew old.

He did not fall endlessly, and he did not hit bottom. He simply stopped falling. When he stopped, he examined the drawings and the spotty gray hands that had made them.

He could not see—

That's all well and good, but really, old man—

that the drawings and the hands did not mean the same thing.

They knew that on one of his rare emergences he rode past Venus, who was playing with her son on the mountain. He wore the cold and dark on his skin, like clothing. He had the cold and dark in his eyes. To Venus, he looked like madness on a horse. Launch one at him, she told her son, because why should that bastard escape desire? The arrow, of course, struck his heart.

What he felt at first was not desire, but the sudden vacuum of his own emptiness, punctured now, and all the world and life he had pushed out of himself rushed back at him, into him, but never filled him. He rode searching, blindly, until he found a woman in a field. She lay on the grass, stretching, and watching the clouds, and the sun lighted her white arms in such a way that he could do nothing but grab her and carry her, screaming, back into the earth.

But in the cavernous darkness, she crumpled. She was a small pale thing curled into itself. He looked at her, touched her, pushed back her hair, and kissed the soft ashen arms. All around, he heard the sad drip of life above ground trickling slowly down to him. She did not wake up and stretch. She only lay there, and he lay on top of her, shivering from the cold.

Our dad bobs down-bayou, too drunk and flabbergasted to fight even the slow, easy current. He tangles up in some hyacinth, grabs hold of stems and thrashes around. My brother and my sister and I watch him thrash around.

Then we feel ourselves surrounded by ourselves, the family around and in line behind, all just watching and waiting. We know that we can and ought to get out of this line now. But where, if not in line? What, if not waiting for an end?

Our dad thrashes in the hyacinth and hollers for somebody to get him a goddamned pole and drag him out.

Let the gars get him, my brother says.

Let the crabs get him, my sister says.

I say, *Ought I to give him some chicken?*

There are no photographs that show details of the celestial object named Pluto's surface. Only the largest formations, the most obvious shadows are visible. There are artists' renderings, though: icy surfaces, cold beyond cold, dark beyond dark, the lonely, desolate pair of Pluto and Charon, in shared orbit around a single axis, the white, mechanical dream of a satellite approaching.

We make drawings, as though imagining and rendering might

contract the distance: we might look back to where Earth should be, and everything we knew before, in its tight familiar orbit, and see nothing.

You are only your shadows. You are only the shadow you cast on me. When the sun moves, and the shadows shift, I'll look where you were and realize that the marks on paper are a false record.

You are only the scent of you in the breeze under this tree. Now that I breathed you in and breathed you out—

and I find myself still breathing—

Mr. A

Having disembarked, clown car–style, from two rented minivans, the twenty-three performers of ACT! Theatre for Kids begin their duckling march across the college quads. The line of child actors draws stares and hoots. They stop conversations. And Julie—the longest-serving (or *longest-surviving,* as Mr. A likes to say) company member—feels a new shiver of embarrassment.

Other troupes here at the state theater conference move in loose agglomerations, with uniforms of sagging jeans, black T-shirts, and bandannas, sporting downy whiskers and ponytails. They joke and shout and curse and cavort. They smoke. Probably they even drink, on the sly. But not so the fifteen girls and eight boys of ACT!, who range in age from five to eighteen and are at all times lined up from tallest to shortest. Attired in pressed khaki pants (except for Julie, who wears a khaki ankle-length skirt), tucked-in T-shirts, and, tied around their waists in this ninety-five-degree heat, shiny red nylon jackets embossed across the back with the ACT! logo, they sing as they promenade—show tunes, vaudeville ditties—Julie's voice the loudest and clearest of all. She has been belting out hymns with her Pentecostal church choir since she was six years old. She is now almost seventeen.

At the head of their line struts J. J. Abrusley, the beloved, the indulgent, the scornful "Mr. A," their gallant captain, their pied piper, small and dapper, straight-backed and trim, extending an arm left or right to steer his trusty procession. His head swivels on a tiny neck, mounted on shoulders made straighter and wider by the stiff pads in his sport coat. Sometimes he turns around to face his charges, his backward stride graceful and confident. In a voice as pinched and reedy as a kazoo, he calls out marching songs. Five bodies ahead of Julie, Jabowen, seventeen and tall and slim, with a bouncing, joyous gait, leads the line of kids. At the rear, Mr. A's mother, Mother A, designated chaperone for the girls, rifles through her enormous purse for tissues, lotion, the crumpled campus map.

All of this—the lockstep marching, the matching clothes, the raising of hands to speak—seemed reasonable back at the rehearsal space this morning, no doubt a necessity for an undertaking such as this, the first of several long-weekend jaunts, the brave inception of a summer tour across the state of Louisiana. When they assembled this morning in the parking lot of the shopping plaza in Lake Charles, where ACT! has a storefront between a ladies' fashion outlet and J. J.'s Food Mart (owned and operated by Mr. A's parents and named, long ago, for the infant Mr. A), they felt every bit like soldiers off to a righteous war. Mr. A moved down the line of kids, addressing each in turn with a gentle clasp of a shoulder or elbow. He looked every kid in the eyes, called each one, warmly, *babe.* Meanwhile Mother A, in her meticulously fluffed silver bouffant and purple tracksuit, ticked off names on a roster and collected permission slips.

This is a new development, this touring business, an expansion of the little company, which until now was limited to a rented auditorium in an abandoned, dilapidated school or to guerrilla-style productions at the mall. But they made a bit of a name for themselves last fall doing whistle-stop campaign performances for now-Governor (again) Edwin Edwards, and with political connections and a new influx of tuition funds, they are taking this show on the road.

This first trip includes the conference in Lafayette and then a New Orleans water park, where they will perform their repertoire of show tunes and Shakespeare for the dripping, shouting, lemonade-sucking hordes loosed from school. Because Julie has been around the longest, she takes charge of practical details like loading luggage and keeping five-year-olds in check. But she didn't sign up to be Mr. A's assistant, and it's been wearing thin.

More than that, while she was loading duffels into the van this morning, she overheard two of the mothers in the parking lot.

"J. J. always picks a favorite," said one.

The other one laughed, and something in that laugh, or maybe just the fact of it, rankled Julie.

Now they are waiting along the wall outside the college

auditorium where they will soon perform their Shakespeare montage. Everyone, even the smallest kid, has a bit. There are very short fragments from *The Tempest, Hamlet, Romeo and Juliet,* and the sonnets, a smattering of just about everything, with some basic facts about the Bard thrown in, less to provide context than to give the youngest children something easy to say. The centerpiece is the strangulation scene from Act V, Scene 2, of *Othello,* with Jabowen as Othello to Julie's Desdemona. Jabowen is the first and only black boy ever to join the company, and Mr. A has seized upon the opportunity.

At the front of the line, Jabowen and Mr. A are talking. Or, more than talking, really. Julie has noticed this before—it's impossible to miss—but today it worries her more deeply than she can quite admit. Jabowen and Mr. A bend toward each other, Mr. A's hand cupping the back of Jabowen's neck, Jabowen's head angled down to Mr. A's, their foreheads nearly touching, eyes locked. Mr. A's feet do an abbreviated box step and his hips shift this way and that while Jabowen stands perfectly still. It is fascinating to watch them, though it ignites a complicated pilot light of jealousy in Julie. What is happening between them is very strange but also nearly beautiful.

Under an oak tree nearby, some teenagers in ripped-up jeans and flannels have been smoking hand-rolled cigarettes and running lines too loudly. "What the fuck!" one is shouting. "What bus did *you* get off of, we're here to fucking *sell. Fuck* marshaling the leads. What the fuck talk is that?"

The little kids down the line look nervously at one another and then at Julie, who shares their anxiety but says,

"Don't listen. Just ignore them." Julie, who, no matter the context, will cringe from her high-spirited peers as from a nest of vipers, wishes she wasn't fearful, but having spent so little time in the world outside her Pentecostal congregation, she knows that she cannot tell vipers from squirrels, danger from fun. And what frightens her more than the danger itself is her own incapacity to see it.

A middle-schooler tells a younger kid, "I don't think those are *regular* cigarettes." Up near the front of the line, Monique, a sixteen-year-old with permed hair, a raspy voice, and a wild energy that intimidates Julie, stuffs her fist between her teeth and shudders with stifled mirth. Under the tree, the teenagers pause in their rehearsal and gawk back at the trail of scandalized kids and the man and boy at the head of the line in their wonderful and disquieting private dance. Mr. A and Jabowen, in each other's thrall, notice none of this.

When, a moment later, the eight-year-old Blaine wanders dreamily out of line to examine a dead pigeon that rests, with its neck twisted, in the grass, Mr. A breaks away from Jabowen and rushes over to scare the wayward boy back into place.

Jabowen approaches Julie and takes hold of her elbow. "Mr. A wants us to run *Out, strumpet,*" he says. He tugs her gently away from the wall. All heads turn to watch.

Jabowen is distracted and will not look her in the eye. It was difficult to get him to commit to the smothering. In the first rehearsals he would bellow, *It is too late,* and palm Julie's face like he was closing the lid of a Tupperware. Finally they decided strangulation would be easier than smothering, which seemed to require a pillow, and Jabowen would come at her neck, his narrow palms and long fingers opening like a Venus flytrap. She grew intimately acquainted with his hands, which were warm and papery, tactful. He would administer the strangling as deliberately and gently as a doctor, pressing his fingers to her collarbone and tensing the muscles in his arms. Julie would take hold of his slender wrists and thrash, desperate-seeming but controlled.

Now they square off like wrestlers and drop their heads, a deep pause and self-collection, a summoning of the essences of Othello and Desdemona. Jabowen counts down from three. Their eyes meet. In Jabowen's, there is an angry flash, a ferocity. He steps forward and again grabs Julie's elbow, violently this time. She shrinks from him first and then falls upon his chest. His free hand burrows into her mass of hair, yanks a handful, pulls hard so her face tilts to his. She has worked up some tears, though mostly it's the pain in her scalp that brings them on.

"Out, strumpet! weep'st thou for him to my face?" Jabowen sighs. He tips his head back and lowers his eyelids, like a jeweler appraising a stone.

"O, banish me, my lord, but kill me not!"

"Down, strumpet!"

"Kill me to-morrow, let me live to-night!"

"Nay, an' you strive—"

Their faces are so close they are sharing breath, and, for Julie, they are together again in the costume closet, that day last month, when, in the fusty, close quarters, amid the reek of stale sweat and old shoes, they could not keep themselves from one awkward and somehow belligerent kiss, Julie's first.

She frees herself from his insistent hands. "But half an hour!" she says.

"Being done, there is no pause."

"But while I say one prayer!"

"It is too late." He pounces upon her.

She thrashes and hisses, "O Lord, Lord, Lord!"

And it is done. She goes limp in his arms. Applause breaks out in the line, the other children nodding.

"Again!" Mr. A shouts.

When they finally take the stage for their performance, there is tittering in the audience, some merciful shushing, but when it is done, when Desdemona has expired, there is unreadable silence. Julie pulls away from Jabowen and blinks into the darkness beyond the stage. A kid rises in the third row. He whoops and claps and whoops again. The girl next to him laughs and tugs at his shirt tail, but then another kid stands, and a few more here and there, then the whole audience is up, clapping and whooping. The little kids in the company join Julie and Jabowen onstage, where they wave, curtsy, and blow kisses. This is what they've been taught to do. They can't hear the mockery in all the applause, but Julie's face heats up.

Jabowen's warm, dry hand finds Julie's; he laces his fingers with hers and squeezes, continues to squeeze, leans into her ear and says, "Philistines." He sweeps their arms up and pulls Julie down with him into a deep and generous bow.

At the first motel, and at each motel thereafter, Mr. A has made reservations for only two rooms, one for the boys and one for the girls. They are on a tight budget, after all. While

Julie, Jabowen, and Mother A hustle the kids and their duffels and sleeping bags from van to room, Mr. A creates a diversion at the front desk, asking for directions to elaborately out-of-the-way landmarks and pretending confusion at every step until all the clerks have gathered around to argue among themselves. Thus the covey of children passes unnoticed into their overfull quarters.

In the girls' room, Julie faces the strategic problem of sleeping space for sixteen bodies. Mother A is no help at all; when it becomes clear that her spatial awareness is entirely distorted, that in each instance little girls are much bigger and areas much smaller than she estimates them to be, Mother A retreats to the bathroom, refusing to help in the one way she possibly could—by asking her son to please, oh please, for heaven's sake, reserve another room.

No matter how Julie configures the space, there is always one girl left with nowhere to sleep. In what seems the best possible arrangement, she and Mother A will share one bed with the tiniest girl, and four small- to medium-sized girls will share the other. The rest are assigned to every bit of floor space, including the entryway, a fire hazard to be sure. But what to do with number sixteen? The tub is considered, and the bathroom floor. Finally, Monique suggests that moving the little table and chairs to the boys' room would free up just enough space. Julie takes up the table, and Monique picks up the chairs.

The boys' room is bigger, Julie notices as soon as she enters—longer by at least four feet, wider by perhaps a foot or two. The beds are luxurious queens instead of fulls. Duffels and sleeping bags are piled in a tidy pyramid against one wall. On the table is a stack of board games: Life, Scrabble, Sorry!, Clue.

Six boys sit cross-legged on the floor in an orderly row, and the boy who has opened the door for Julie and Monique returns to his place on the end. They are playing some sort of word game, nickering like dolphins at Mr. A, who perches on the edge of the bed, Jabowen at his side. "*Baboon* but not *monkey,*" says Mr. A. "*Warrior* but not *chief.*"

Julie peeks over the rim of the tabletop she is clutching to her body and waits for Mr. A to give the girls his attention. Monique is not so patient. She bumps one of the chairs intentionally against the wall before she sets it down, then clears her throat.

"Jules!" says Mr. A, cheery. "What do you need, babe?"

Without hesitation, Monique, a hand on her defiantly cocked hip, answers first, explaining their predicament.

Mr. A orders two of the older boys—not Jabowen—to stack the table and chairs out of the way, in the corner of the room, and when they have done so and have resumed their places on the floor, he pats the bed next to him and tells the girls, "Stay a minute. See if you can figure this out."

Although Monique is fast and lithe and more ruthless, Julie, a couple of steps closer to the bed, has the advantage of proximity and nabs the place at Mr. A's left hand, which means Monique must join the boys on the floor.

Without explanation, Mr. A continues the game. "*Actresses* but not *actors. Othello* but not *Iago.*"

Blaine raises his hand. "*Black* but not *white*?"

"Nope, wrong again," Mr. A says.

Julie is too close to him to watch his face, which has grown an uncharacteristic stubble that extends down his neck, where the skin is red and bumpy. Instead she looks at his lap and, just on the other side of his lap, Jabowen's. Mr. A's legs, thin as pipes, are crossed at the thighs, his hands resting, one atop the other, on the uppermost knee. The suspended foot bounces restlessly, making the bedsprings squeak. Jabowen sits with his legs spread wide and reclines slightly, propped on his arms.

"*Swimming* but not *drowning*," Mr. A says.

Monique shoots her hand up and says, "Does it have something to do with...?" But she trails off.

"Oh!" Jabowen says. "I've got it! *William* but not *Shakespeare*."

"Yes!" Mr. A says. His right hand reaches for Jabowen's left leg and pats it on the thigh. "Exactly!"

"*Appendicitis* but not *cancer*!" Jabowen says.

Mr. A's hand comes to rest—frankly, firmly—just above Jabowen's knee.

Monique tries again. "*Sick* but not *dead*?"

"No, that's not it," Mr. A says, and the hand on Jabowen's thigh gives a little squeeze, then retracts, as if Mr. A has remembered himself.

They go on like this for a while, the boys and Monique offering wrong answers, Mr. A throwing out new examples. Sometimes Jabowen chimes in, and when he does, Mr. A's hand reaches over, comes alive with friendly patting.

"Any ideas, Jules?" Mr. A says.

She feels him looking at her, but she cannot stop watching the hand. Over the hill of Mr. A's crossed knees, Monique is peeping at Julie with one eyebrow theatrically raised and her glossy upper lip in a curl. Julie meets Mr. A's eyes. They are, as always, shockingly blue, direct and perceptive. Jabowen drops flat onto the bed and lolls his head to look at her behind Mr. A. He gives her a warm, flirtatious smile. He seems quite pleased with himself, actually.

"What are the rules?" Julie says to Jabowen. And then to Mr. A: "I don't understand the rules."

If Julie's parents knew the iniquities to which the theater has tempted their daughter—for instance, changing out of her pious to-the-ankle denim skirt and into a pair of knee-length shorts on arrival at rehearsals, or being made by Mr. A to die again and again at the hands of a boy, a black boy no less, with each little death arousing concupiscence—they would have removed her from ACT! long ago. But they stay far away from ACT! Never in her five years with Mr. A have Julie's parents seen her perform. For them the public display of her talent is confined to church services, where she sings hymns beautifully, with great drama even, but only for God's glory. Outside of church, performance is, if not strictly forbidden, a temptation—to lust, to pride.

But so complete was the trust Julie's parents had in their daughter, so good and smart and sensible a girl was she, and so flattered were they in spite of themselves that their girl at only twelve was cast in the lead of a play on her very first try, that they gave in after some pleading and a promise that Julie's involvement with ACT! and Mr. A was to remain a secret from their Pentecostal congregation with the same urgency as a pregnancy begotten out of wedlock.

There had been some trouble with her grandmother, though. On the night before Julie's first performance, the family was seated around the table offering up the dinnertime prayer when MeeMom raised herself out of her chair. She held her hands out to Julie, palms open, then let them rise slowly upward as though she were testing for rain. "My baby," she said. "My baby, Julie." She was waiting for the prayer to come, pleading with her granddaughter and with God, and then the prayer did come. "The Lord God has given you to us, Julie, He has laid you on my bosom like a sleeping babe, and I ask Him to help me protect you." She came around the table and pulled Julie toward her soft belly, held her there for a while and stroked her hair, tucked strands of it behind her ears, petted her face. Julie's father and mother kept their eyes on their forks. MeeMom pressed her hands to either side of Julie's head, muffling her ears, and said, very quietly, "I ask you, Jesus, to cleanse my Julie in Your blood. Wash her clean in Your blood, the blood of Jesus Christ. Release her from the devils within her. Fill her to overflowing with the gift of the Holy Ghost, let it fill her."

And the prayer, a muted buzz in Julie's ears, vibrated, escalated, then left language behind. The tongues of angels overtook the deficient tongue of man, and the pulsing through the hands of her grandmother—her own beloved MeeMom, who had taught her and loved her and always been kind—the seeming pulse of grace itself, awakened something angry and latent in Julie's chest, a demon, maybe, hammering to get out.

The next day she went early to rehearsal and told Mr. A,

weeping, that she had to quit. For her grandmother, whom she loved, she had to quit.

He stood from behind his desk, planted his hands presidentially upon it, and leaned forward, his sport coat spreading out from his small frame like the agitated frills of a lizard. "That's exactly why I don't go in for all that Holy Spirit gobbledy-gobble," he said. "These are the same people who would burn every volume of Shakespeare if they got the chance. Philistines, Julie! These people are philistines." He ringed an arm around her shoulders as they walked down the hall to the rehearsal room and, drawing her close, said in her ear, to the jittery, jumping thing that her grandmother could not cast out: "Mr. A is telling you, and what Mr. A tells you, you can believe: You. Are. No. Demon."

That day in rehearsal, when Mr. A, leading the chorus of nonsense phrases that would unravel their tongues for performance, raised his hands to heaven, clapped them over his head, and whooped like a zealot—"Canada Molega Rimini Brindisi! Canada Molega Rimini Brindisi! Nagasakiiiiiiiii! Hallelujah! Praise the Lord Jesus!"—Julie, like the others, laughed and answered the call.

Back in the girls' bathroom, Julie crouches on the lid of the toilet with a stopwatch in hand. Each girl has two minutes for a shower. Julie gives a warning at one minute and another with thirty seconds remaining. At two minutes, if the curtain has not been shoved aside and a naked body toweled off and wrapped up of its own accord, Julie threatens, then pulls the curtain open herself, shuts off the water, and drags an occasionally still soapy and trembling little girl onto a soaking rug to towel and wrap her herself. Outside, Mother A presents each one with her neatly folded panties and pajamas. They must all be clean and ready for bed by nine. Thus spake Mr. A.

For herself, Julie will reserve the luxury of a morning shower, before the other girls are up, when she can sufficiently lather, rinse, and coil into a bun the thick mane of hair that hangs past her waist, and see to certain aspects of feminine hygiene that simply cannot be addressed, along with everything else, in two minutes. Under the cover of predawn darkness, her hypocrisy will go mostly unnoticed.

It is awkward, she knows, to claim this privilege when a few of the other girls, also in their mid- to late teens, have the need but no recourse. Monique, though, pushes past the two-minute mark every time. While Julie, sweating, wipes steam away from the face of the stopwatch, Monique says, "What's the deal, do you think, with Jabowen and Mr. A?"

"One minute left," Julie says.

The rush of water changes tone and there's a sudden spatter against the curtain. Julie wipes the damp from her face with a piece of toilet paper, which, when she drops it into the trash, is smeared with creamy brown makeup—another taboo, like shorts and dancing, in her family home.

"It's starting to give me the creeps," says Monique.

"Thirty seconds."

"This whole thing, actually. Doesn't it feel sometimes like a. Like we're in a."

"Fifteen seconds."

"Like a cult?" The curtain moves aside a little and a

furtive foot emerges, mounts the rim of the tub. Julie thinks Monique is going to give her a break and exit the shower without being told, but instead she reaches out with a dripping hand and roots around in the cosmetics bag on the counter until she finds a razor.

Julie inspects the watch. Time's up. More than up. She gives Monique another minute, and at the end of that minute Monique is still shaving, so Julie gives her one more, two. Even three. "It's been two minutes," she says, finally. "You have to get out."

"Oh, please," Monique says and does not get out.

At one in the morning, Julie is still awake. Mother A, herself equipped with earplugs, is snoring, deeply, strangely, loudly, on the other side of Julie's bed. The little five-year-old is curled up like a bean against Julie's back, drawing closer and closer with every hour and pushing Julie farther toward the edge. The room is too warm, heavy with a damp, swampy odor. The buzzing of so many bodies in sleep is its own kind of chaos, a swelling of potential energy, a spring stretched to its limit.

At 1:15 there is a knock on the door—a light, shy tapping with the tips of fingers, one, two, three. At first Julie thinks she has imagined this, or that the sound has come from somewhere inside the throbbing room. But then, a moment later, there it is again, a little louder this time. Julie swings her feet to the floor and barely misses Monique's sprawled arm. She picks her way around bodies, testing each step with her toes before planting her foot. There is a third knock just as she reaches the door.

It is Blaine. He looks frightened. "I need to pee," he says, and grabs at the flannel crotch of his pajama pants. He casts an anxious glance over his shoulder, as though he expects to have been followed, and does a little dance. "I need to *pee.*"

"What's wrong with the toilet in your room?"

"Mr. A is in there."

"Did you knock?"

"He said go away."

"Good grief, Blaine. If he catches you in the hallway, you'll be in serious trouble."

"He's been in there forever." Blaine bends into a crouch, then stands and again checks behind him for pursuers. "Jabowen is in there too," he says. "I mean, I think he is. He's not in bed."

"Maybe he took a walk or something. Maybe he went to get ice. Or a snack."

"Julie, *please* can I pee?"

What else can she do but let him in? She doesn't follow him, though. Instead she goes to the door of the boys' room and finds it propped open with a sneaker. She pushes it open just enough to poke her head through. A sliver of light spills out under the bathroom door, only a couple of steps from the hallway. Julie slips inside the room and presses her ear against the bathroom door.

There is low talking with long, pensive pauses. She can't make out the words, but she recognizes their tones and textures, their deep, serious hum. It is indeed Jabowen and Mr. A. When the door to the room swings open behind her, she starts and nearly cries out. It is only Blaine. They squeeze past each other—she to the hallway, he to bed—averting their eyes.

At breakfast, Jabowen looks ragged in a nonspecific way, his eyes puffy and blank, preoccupied with the heap of pancakes and the halved egg burrito he is sharing with Mr. A. The boys have all been served and are seated at a long bank of two-person tables, but the girls are still trickling through the line, confounding the clerks with elaborate orders and last-minute corrections.

Julie, who was wide awake when her alarm went off at six and feels as though she's spent the night in the trunk of a rotted-out tree, has been standing at the counter, helping the little ones with their cash, matching receipts to trays, so hungry that she's light-headed. She's keeping an eye on the open chair at Mr. A's table, and as each girl goes off to find a seat, her head floods with a desperate rush of blood. There is an answer at that table to the question of the closed bathroom door; there will be signs, and if she doesn't get to that table soon she will be excluded irreversibly from whatever is happening between Jabowen and Mr. A. Meanwhile she mixes up orders, she miscounts bills.

When Monique, the last in line, reaches the counter, she says, "Julie, you're purple!" She orders a breakfast sandwich, pancakes, hash browns, an extra side of bacon, and a vanilla shake. "God, I'm starving," she says.

If none of the other girls has the gumption to claim the seat across from Mr. A, deterred by an instinctive and inviolable sense of the troupe's pecking order, Monique certainly does. And in fact, Julie, now so flustered that she orders nothing but coffee and a biscuit, stares after Monique as she flounces down the aisle directly to Mr. A's table and claims the empty chair as hers, exactly as she did in the high school cafeteria on her first day as a freshman, certain of her place at a table full of cheerleaders and dancers, while Julie, a junior, had been unable in two years to establish herself except in a lonesome corner with kids from her church, better dressed for the prairie than for adolescence. The two girls had known each other from ACT! for a while by then, but when Monique saw Julie in her trailing skirt and grandmotherly bun, she puckered her lips in a smirk and moved on.

Now, though, when Julie finally has her tray in hand, with her sad little breakfast that she doesn't even want, the coveted seat is still empty. Mr. A is waving her over, having shooed Monique to another table.

Jabowen peels back the aluminum lid of an orange juice, concentrating, as careful in this as he is with Desdemona's neck. Just when Julie has decided that he is, for one reason or another, avoiding her eyes, he looks up, twinkle-eyed, grinning. "Straws are for philistines," he says, and takes a deep gulp.

Mr. A swipes a forkful of pancakes off Jabowen's plate and onto Julie's. "You don't have nearly enough to eat there," he says.

Julie says she's not really hungry. She picks up her biscuit and nibbles it, but feels like she'll gag if she tries to swallow. She lifts her napkin to her mouth and discreetly spits the biscuit out.

"Got to keep your strength up, babe," Mr. A says. He takes hold of the nape of her neck and gives it a quick little one-handed massage. "Today's your big New Orleans debut."

For the rest of breakfast, they are all business. They discuss the lineup of songs and skits for their performance later that day—on an outdoor stage at the water park—and Mr. A makes a list on a napkin, which he entrusts to Julie. He calls Mother A to their table and confers with her over directions to the water park and the motel.

When the other kids, high on syrup and surreptitiously ordered soft drinks, get a little raucous, Mr. A beats his keys on the table and growls, "Excuse me! Where do you think you are?"

Jabowen and Julie sit at attention, waiting for the next command. In other words, everyone behaves in a way that is exactly normal and Julie begins to doubt what she has seen, or, rather, begins to acknowledge her imperfect understanding of it.

At the end of the meal, Mr. A and Mother A conduct one group to the bathrooms, leaving Julie and Jabowen in charge of the others, still seated and restless. Julie is flattening and crumpling, flattening and crumpling the discarded wrapper of a straw, and Jabowen is gazing out the window at the bright, hot day and the trucks trundling by on the interstate. Suddenly, he reaches across the table and stops her hands. He takes away the straw wrapper, balls it up, and lobs it into Monique's frizzed-up hair. Monique is drawing something on a napkin for a small crowd of kids and doesn't notice.

"Why are you acting so weird?" he asks Julie.

"I'm not acting weird. Why are you acting weird?"

"I'm not." His eyes get the ferocious gleam again. He

looks over his shoulder toward the bathroom, she assumes for Mr. A, and she tugs a napkin from their decimated serving trays and starts ripping it carefully to shreds.

After their kiss in the costume closet, Julie and Jabowen contrived to see each other outside rehearsal. Julie, wearing her best church skirt, told her parents she was needed at ACT!, and Jabowen picked her up from school in his car.

"You drive a Mercedes?" she said.

It was a little nicked up and had so much trash on the passenger's seat and floorboard—discarded T-shirts, crushed soda cans, crumpled and foot-printed essays, tests, and newspapers—that he had to shovel armloads into the back seat before he would let her in, but it was a Mercedes nonetheless.

"Sorry," he kept saying. "I'm a slob. Sorry."

"Is this your dad's car?"

"Used to be. He's sporting an S-Class now."

He drove her across town to a neighborhood she had heard about but never visited, regarded as it was by her parents and grandmother with such pious contempt and suspicion (and some latent awe, sure) that it glowed in a radioactive nimbus of taboo. Here the grand houses of local celebrities—a television newscaster, a restaurateur, the mayor—lined the nicest stretch of lakefront in town. The petrochemical plants where her father worked were so far away that they were just a low, craggy shadow, hardly visible across the water. Jabowen slowed in front of a massive white mansion set too close to the road, crammed onto a piece of property just wider than the house itself. It loomed above them like the face of a cliff.

"Isn't this wild?" he said. "It's an exact replica of Tara."

Julie stared at him, her face blank.

"The plantation house?" he said. "From *Gone with the Wind*?"

"I haven't seen that movie."

"You haven't?" He was disproportionately incredulous. "You *have* to see it. Ask Mr. A. He'll tell you how great it is." Then he turned into the driveway. "Real estate is so cheap in Lake Charles, it's unbelievable. And anyway, my dad thinks it's hilarious."

"Why?" Julie said.

"It's kind of sweet, I guess, but you really have no sense of irony."

Inside, Jabowen took Julie's hand to lead her across a cavernous foyer, up a spiral staircase, down a hallway as long as a small hotel's—and with as many closed doors—and finally into his room, which, unlike his car, was neat as a pin and smelled like sandalwood and pickles.

"My parents aren't here," he said. "We have the whole house."

He showed her the things in his room that mattered to him: a trophy for dramatic interp, a funny birthday card from Mr. A, a carved wooden mask that he got on a trip to Nigeria with his father. On his bedside table was a photo of him and his parents, the three of them draped in bright African prints. They posed in front of two thatch-roofed huts, all smiles, with a crowd of villagers lined up behind them, gazing frankly at the camera. His mother's head was wrapped elaborately in some kind of scarf.

"Is this where your parents are from?"

He gave a petulant little huff and said that Nigeria had been a business trip. His dad, who was a bigwig at CITGO, was from right here in Lake Charles. His mom, a high school math teacher, was from D.C.

Jabowen sat down on the bed next to Julie. "You have little hairs on your cheek," he said and brushed his fingers over them. He leaned in and touched her ear with his nose, then with his tongue.

She jerked away at first, but then she let him, and liked it. By the time the shadows of evening started to creep in, her hair was unwound from its bun and her long skirt was tangled up at her knees. She straightened herself in the bathroom, and Jabowen led her double-time down the great, curving staircase as though it were no more than a fire escape. He drove her to the ACT! parking lot, where she'd told her father to pick her up at six, and he waited with her there, gentlemanly, for the fifteen minutes until her father arrived. He opened the door of her father's truck for her, then he reached across the cab, which smelled like gasoline and sweat, to shake her father's hand. Jabowen's Mercedes was the only other car in the lot, and her father looked at it a good long time before finally pulling out.

"Where'd he get that car?" he said. It wasn't really a question. "I didn't know you were spending time with a crowd like that."

The next night, while Julie was washing the dishes from supper, Jabowen called. Her hands dripped on the floor as she cradled the phone between shoulder and chin. Her mother and grandmother were in the living room, building care packages of pamphlets and chocolate for prisoners who had repented and accepted Christ. They had the TV turned to one of their favorite preachers, and Julie could hear the angry, damning cadences of the man's voice but not the content of the sermon.

"We can't do that anymore," she said quietly. The door from the kitchen to the garage was open, and her father was out there clattering around in his toolbox for something to fix the refrigerator, which that day had leaked a puddle of icy water across the kitchen floor.

Jabowen breathed into the phone. "Don't you like me?"

"I like you."

"Then why? Is it because I'm black?"

"Of course not," she said. How could she pull apart all the layers of prohibition, much less list them over the phone? Especially when the prohibitions were so at odds with her desires. "It's just—Mr. A wouldn't like it." Before Jabowen could argue, she hung up.

That was only two weeks ago. They have hardly spoken to each other since, except as Othello and Desdemona.

On the trip from Lafayette to New Orleans, Julie rides in the second van, driven by the easily rattled Mother A. Whenever Mr. A veers into the passing lane to speed around a big rig, Mother A says, "Oh, J. J., oh, J. J., God help us," before she jerks her van behind his and creeps ever so slowly past the truck, lingering dangerously in its blind spot. A few times Mr. A has slowed, waved them alongside, and motioned for Mother A to lower a window so that his van can serenade hers with songs from the ACT! vaudeville routine—*Hello my baby, hello my honey, hello my ragtime gal!*

"Use every minute!" he shouts, and motors ahead.

Julie, who does not want the responsibility of soothing Mother A's nerves for two hours, has let Monique take the shotgun seat. Monique's long legs are draped across the dashboard and she's reading a magazine. When Mother A gets flustered, Monique says, without looking up, "Settle down, Mother A, settle down."

Her empty stomach heaving and groaning, Julie sits in the stale air of the very back, at the end of a row of the little ones, who have, after an hour on the road, mostly fallen asleep. In front of her, a fourteen-year-old girl and an eight-year-old boy are turned toward each other, slapping hands in a complicated rhythm and chanting. When one of them misses a beat, they dissolve into giggles and paw at each other.

By the time they have pushed through New Orleans traffic and reached the water park, everyone, especially Julie, is thirsty. But they are scheduled to perform in less than an hour, and since they will first need to visit a restroom, there is no time to stop for drinks. Mr. A enlists one of the boys to carry the jug of Gatorade from the van and one of the girls ferries the Dixie cups. Rations will be distributed when they get to the stage. They assemble in their usual line and trace their way through the maze of paths, twice making wrong turns and stopping to consult a map on which distances are not at all accurate. Waterslides and chutes in primary colors tower all around them, some several stories high, and from every direction come delighted screams, sudden splashes.

They are moving fast, and Mr. A has not once turned around. He charges ahead, yelling over his shoulder for everyone to keep up.

Jabowen strides easily at the head of the line. Monique traipses after him. Behind Julie, the boy with the Gatorade stumbles and drops the jug, has to chase it as it rolls into the grass on the side of the path.

At the back of the line, Mother A, bent forward with the effort of keeping up, says again and again, "Lord, this heat!" and fans herself with the folded map.

Julie's lips have started to parch; her stomach has not recovered from the ride. Every time she passes a kiosk selling lemonade and slushies, or steps over a puddle of water in the path, she is acutely aware of a clenching, twisting fist around her kidneys.

Once, she calls out to Mr. A, but he barks, "Not now!" without glancing back, as though she were just any other kid in the line.

When they reach a restroom, Julie is of course in charge of getting everyone through in a timely fashion. She stands near the row of sinks, ushering little girls into empty stalls, helping them with buttons and snaps and shoelaces that have come loose, reminding them to wash their hands. If there is ever a moment when no one is entering or leaving a stall, she tries to get a drink of water from the sink. But because the faucet knob is spring-loaded it will run only as long as she holds it on, which means she can collect barely a sip of water at a time in one shallow cupped palm, or else she must bend down to the stream and slurp.

With only ten minutes until the performance, they finally reach the stage. Although there are tree-shaded benches and lawns all around, the stage itself is in full sunlight, and now, at nearly two o'clock in the afternoon, the temperature is creeping toward 100 degrees. Mercifully, Mr. A has them sit under the trees. To Jabowen he hands the Gatorade, to Julie the Dixie cups.

As she moves toward the clusters of kids, seated Indian-style on the shaded grass, her skin feels like wool; the heat was bad before but now it is unbearable. She tries to hand a cup to the kid she knows is sitting right at her feet, but suddenly she cannot see him. A blackness has crept across the ground and swallowed Julie to the waist. She hears herself say, "Where are you?" Someone else says, "You should sit down."

And then she is swallowed completely.

When she comes to, she thinks at first that she is at a church picnic, that she has been napping on a blanket with her MeeMom. The branches of a tree spread above her. A chorus of song wafts not far away. But the presence she thought was her grandmother is not her grandmother at all. It's Mother A, fanning her with the map, laying a cool, wet handkerchief on her forehead.

Julie leans up on her elbows. The kids of ACT! are already on, and Mr. A is hovering near the stage. A crowd has gathered in the bleachers. Jabowen and Monique come forward while the rest of the kids recede.

"I told him we ought to take you to the hospital," Mother A says, "but he won't listen." This is the first word of criticism Mother A has ever had for her son. She hands Julie a cup of Gatorade and refills it three times. "If it was that young man laying here in the grass right now, there would've been a doctor called, I can tell you."

154

Julie drags herself to a sitting position against the trunk of the tree. Onstage, Monique thrashes, her tiny throat pinched between Jabowen's hands, then crumples to the ground.

"He wouldn't want to jeopardize the money, is what it is." Julie stares at Mother A, perplexed.

"From Jabowen's daddy. For the company." He's the one paying for all of this.

The show is done and the band of kids comes laughing and wound-up back to the shade under the trees. The little ones surround Julie, overly attentive, until Mr. A shoos them back into formation and squats by her side.

"How do you feel, babe?" he says. He slides his left hand under the back of her neck, lifts her long hair. His right hand moves up and down her arm, shoulder to elbow.

Is it the same? Julie wonders. Is the way he touches her exactly the same as how he touches Jabowen?

Mr. A takes his left hand from her neck, moves the right hand to her thigh. He pats quickly three times, already distracted by what's happening among the kids, in this case Jabowen and Monique, who are replaying the Othello scene, but in reverse.

"But half an hour," Jabowen squeaks. "But while I say one prayer!"

Monique, in a deep bass, bellows, "It is too late!" and lunges for Jabowen's throat.

Mr. A has promised them pizza after they check in to the next motel and rest for a few hours. Later, too, they will call their parents, to assure them that no one is dead in a ditch along Interstate 10. For now, Mother A has gone down to the motel restaurant for a cup of coffee and some time alone with a ladies' magazine, and Julie has been sleeping, finally, on one of the beds while the other girls color or read or pass notes and whisper or doze off themselves.

Julie is sleeping so soundly, in fact, that she does not hear the knock at the door, the filing in of seven slouching boys who have been expelled from their own motel room. The boys find places as best they can in the overcrowded room, in corners, under the table, one of them on the edge of the bed where Julie is sleeping, and this is what finally wakes her.

Puffy-eyed, muddled, she sits upright, pinches her eyebrows together. "What are you doing here?" she asks the boy, then takes in the room. "What are you *all* doing here?"

Monique is standing in front of the mirror, hand on a cocked hip, watching her own reflection. "Mr. A sent them here." She raises one leg in an arabesque, nearly kicking another girl in the face. The boys stare at Monique's lifted leg. Someone suggests a game of charades.

Julie doesn't even bother to think of a pretense. She kicks off the covers, picks her way around the kids on the floor, and pounds down the walkway to the boys' room. She knocks, hard.

Jabowen opens the door in his boxers and undershirt. "Oh," he says. "It's you." He moves aside to let her in.

Mr. A is lounging on the bed. He too has shed his sport coat and pants, but wears an ACT! T-shirt many sizes too big and boxers with yellow happy faces. Skinny and startled, he reminds Julie of a hermit crab plucked from its shell. Before him is the Scrabble board. Tiles are scattered across the quilt and he is dropping them by the handful into a velvet bag.

"Scrabble! Come sit down, babe." Mr. A pats the bed. "You can still get in on this game."

Jabowen hands her the velvet bag. "Draw your tiles," he says.

They settle together on the bed. Julie draws her tiles, as she is told, and arranges them on a rack: *Q T N A Y D C*. She knows there must be a word in there to lay on the board between Jabowen's and Mr. A's, and she shuffles the tiles around trying to see it. Mr. A is prompting her, gently teasing, talking a little trash. Jabowen stares seriously down at his own tiles. Her bare legs and Jabowen's bare legs and Mr. A's bare and hairy legs are all at angles on the bed, nearly but not touching. Jabowen is rattling tiles in his hand, impatient. Julie stares at her own.

She stares so long that Mr. A leans over to help. He points to an available *S* on the board. "*NASTY*," he says.

Now Jabowen leans in too and says, "*DYNAST. ANTSY. STAND. SAND. STAY.* Just pick one and play it, Jules." He finds Mr. A's pinkie with his pinkie and strokes it.

She wasn't meant to see.

Or she was and it's nothing. Her tiles blur. *By heaven, I saw my handkerchief in 's hand!* But seeing is not all. She has learned this, at least, from Shakespeare and from church. One can see indeed yet perceive not, hear indeed yet understand not, divide the world in accordance with rules—*Othello* but not *Desdemona*, divine *messengers* but not *demons*, *culottes* but not *shorts*, *affluent* but not *white*, *beardless* but not *vulnerable*, *innocent* but not *chaste*, *passion* but not *lust*—yet fathom not the division.

"Double letters," Julie says. "The rule is double letters."

Jabowen and Mr. A stare blankly at her, then Jabowen, understanding, reaches over, pats her on the head. "Very good, kid," he says, "but that was two days ago. We've moved on to Scrabble. For heaven's sake, play your word."

Cut Off, Louisiana:
A Ghost Story

WHAT TO EAT WHEN THERE'S NOTHING TO EAT

How could you, Mark Twain? How could you lie in that bed-out-of-nowhere, in my kitchen suddenly, covered to your chin with quilt and comfort, and suggest that I feed my family raw turnips?

"I've got nothing to put with those turnips," I said. "No salt. No onions. Nothing. They won't make much of a soup."

You said, "Don't cook them, Marie. Your family won't know the difference."

How could I set my table, on your word, for a five-course meal? And how, then, could you titter through your mustache while Ulysse commended the pork roast; my seven

159

children the gumbo, greens, and cobbler; and no one asked where or how, or thought of turnips?

Then night after night, when one and then another and another of the children took to bed with tummies swollen and hard (as turnips), and mouths round for complaining, but mute—only burps popping like bubbles from their lips when, one by one, they settled into the straw mattress, deflated of turnip gas and soul—and, Mark Twain, when Ulysse carried the wilted bodies, one every night for a week, and potted them in the mire behind the chicken house while I and my dwindling brood paced the yard where there had been no chickens since fall—

How could you wiggle your toes like that, cozy under your counterpane, delighted?

And when, praying the Our Father at our kitchen table after he buried the last, Ulysse belched at kingdom come, and said, *"Marie, j'mai sent comme ci j'manger trop navet. J'ai de gaz,"** how could I tug at the hairs on the hide seat of my chair and answer him: *It's only grief.* And you, in the corner by the door, bobbing your white head. Even the bedsprings laughed at your joke.

In the morning, Ulysse passed through you in his hat and boots and shabby coat pulled tight across his belly—you, still in your bed, with your nightcap cocked over one eye. He didn't notice you at all. *I'll go till I find work,* he said. Now, even the turnips were gone. *Amen,* I said, as you plucked a button from his coat, as his belly tumbled free, as he tottered

---

* "Marie, I feel like I've eaten too many turnips. I've got gas."

down the road toward town to look for work where there was no work, only mud roads skirting a dead river and branching out into the subtropical everywhere winter.

I prayed, and late afternoon, they started to come. Felicia and Helene and Marie Arceneau and Marie Thibodeau and Ovide Latourneau, all of them, from all over the parish. Père Alceé read psalms and Latourneau pounded the porch posts, three times each, and lit a green candle at my door. The women of the parish piled food on my table: lard, sacks of potatoes, smoked sausage, ti' salée, boudin, fig preserves, a chicken, carrots, onions, rice, and rice, and rice, and rice. LeLe Balais brought a cornbread two miles on foot with a baby riding her hip.

"*Chère* LeLe, how can you spare it?" I said.

"*C'est rien,*" she said.

The baby, starved dumb in the womb, hid its face in LeLe's hair and moaned while you waved and cooed and made smoke rings with your pipe.

I see you writing in that notebook, laughing while you write. All over the parish, for weeks, I know there's been nothing but turnips. How could you play that giggling, sputtering tune through the comb teeth of your moustache, while I dare not eat a bite, after three days, of this food on my table?

Mark Twain, have you been in their kitchens too?

THE RIVER MOVED

If a farmer, landlocked at the mouth of a horseshoe curve, wants the river at his back door, he might burn a water moccasin from that same river, and spread its ash where he wishes the river to run. He might make a *gris gris* of thirteen pennies, nine cotton seeds, and hair from a black hog, then, under a waning moon, with *gris gris* in hand, summon the river as he would a spirit. He might, at the very least, light a red candle upside down and hope for the best. But the surest way to move a river is to dig a narrow ditch along the neck of the curve—slit it like a throat—and wait for flood.

Your River came through here once, and you on it.

Our grandfathers remembered you, in our town. You, a famous man, a great man—so our grandfathers were told—passed the day with them on their porches. They did not know your name, but you drew eyes, then crowds, when you came ashore, with your madman's hair and imperial air, claiming this River, and all lands drained by it. It was a kindness, a blessing, that you sat with them on their porches.

They told you stories. *Our granddaddy Jean-le-Sot,* they said in French, *he was such a fool—he wanted to hide his gold.* "What I'm gonna do with all this gold?" *he thought.* "Somebody's gonna steal it." *So he got in his pirogue and rowed far out upon the great bayou—the one they call the Mississippi River—and he dumped that sack of gold overboard.* "Now," *he thought,* "how I'm gonna find it again?" *So he put him a big X on the side of that pirogue, right over where he dumped the gold . . .*

They laughed at themselves. They were the fools of their own tales.

You tried your French, too. *"La rivière est large . . ."* you said.

"Ain?" they said.

"La rivière," you said, *"est l-a-r-g-e . . ."*

They shook their heads.

"La rivière est large! La rivière est large! La r-i-v-i-è-r-e . . ."

"Ouais, ouais . . . !"

". . . est . . ."

"Quoi?"

"Dad-blame-it, gentlemen!" you said, without a wink or smile, "I've seen this River so wide it had only one bank." You puffed on your pipe and waited for laughter. You might have been a senator, a judge, the President, mourning the deaths from past floods. They said, *"Ouais,"* and nodded solemnly. You made them the fools of your tales, too. The River, meanwhile, peeked over the neglected levees at the man who flattered its flow and size and lore.

You so charmed the River that, after you had tamped out your pipe, shaken hands with the Frenchmen, and floated on toward New Orleans, the River leapt its banks and flooded our town, searching for you. Water rose above our grandfathers' porches. The animals drowned. The River found the ditch dug by the landlocked farmer and rushed into it, chased after you.

In the morning our town was no longer a River town, swamp up to the porches, our grandparents beset by mosquitoes. Our grandfathers launched their boats into still water.

The River had moved thirty miles farther east.

They say old N'onc Télémaque, returning from the Gulf the night of the flood, took his shrimp boat around the old bend and never found his way home. They say even now you can see him in the swamp, in his boat, tracing a memory of the River, and finding no outlet.

Our grandparents told this story to our mothers and fathers, and then to us. They learned your name, and who you were, from the New Orleans paper that reported the flood. A man named Clemens, or Twain, got his picture on the front page, they said, all because he romanced the River away from them, *à l'anglais.*

N'ONC TÉLÉMAQUE

Our grandmothers remembered the River's tangled banks. At certain stages of the moon, they would trample through, disrobe, dip in—to ease cramps or to conceive, to cure the sun-pain from a day in the fields. The River swept prayers, luck, fertility, beauty, health away from northern women and carried these offerings a thousand miles to our grandmothers. They took the water away in jars to sprinkle on babies. They blessed their husbands' fields and animals. They blessed the doorsteps of their homes.

Then the River moved.

Our grandmothers went to the swamp one summer night, hoping for the same cures from stagnant water. The hyacinth, by then, had grown dense across the water, and anyone who did not know better might have mistaken swamp for field. Anyone who did not know better might have walked across it.

Our grandmothers waded in to their bellies, some plump, some thin, some pregnant. The hyacinth separated, let them pass, then closed again behind them. Tidy greenness swept away the ragged disorder of current. They floated on their backs and thought, *Who needs a river?* Their bodies flashed like swamp fire.

They heard a splash behind a cypress stump. Hyacinth bobbed and parted. They covered their breasts, and thought: *Cocodrie! Ouaouaron! Caouane! Serpent congo!**

An old man sloshed around the stump, waist-deep in swamp water. His hair was knotted and green with slime, his mustache a matted clump on his lip. Behind him, a shrimp boat, draped in nets, tilted out of the muck. Everything smelled of rotten fish.

I followed the glow of le feu follé *to you!* the old man said. *I'd gladly stay lost a hundred years to see so many lovely bottoms.* He laughed and waded toward them, his fingers itching to touch.

Who are you, old man? asked one of the women.

That's just N'onc Télémaque, said my grandmother. Those twitching fingers, like crab claws (now blue), had pinched her bottom often enough. *He won't hurt nobody.*

But when the swamp-blessed mothers gave birth to babies with webs instead of fingers and toes, our grandmothers prayed for the River's return.

SWAMP FIRE

After three days, I stopped praying and rose from my table, swooned from hunger, grabbed my chair for balance. I said, "Mark Twain, I'll undo what you did."

From my cabinet, I took an empty jar (they were all

---

*   Alligator! Bullfrog! Snapping turtle! Moccasin!

empty, the preserves long ago eaten). I stepped over the sacks of potatoes and onions and rice and went into the night the way my husband had gone, toward town, then through town, toward swamp—the heaps of food left to rot on my table.

When I passed the Balais farm, dead as our own, the last land before the swamp, LeLe ran to me with a wool coat and lighted lantern. LeLe wrapped the coat around my shoulders and hung the lantern on my wrist. She said, *Marie, down there is a pirogue. Take it! Watch out for* le feu follé!"

So, in the pirogue, I crossed into a black and silent chaos, an unpredictable stillness. In the circle of lantern light: my bare feet, the jar between them, the rough-cut wood under them keeping me afloat, my push pole planted like a colonial flag in every yard of muck, my gray hands on the push pole, the noise of my wake.

And, beyond the light: what?

Hunger was beyond the light, and grief, the flares of green and blue—*le feu follé*—that weren't light at all, but more like the mind's memory of light, or hope.

Then suddenly, in the light, a man. He stood in the water before the pirogue. His hair was wild, he smelled of shrimp. He said, *Marie, I followed* le feu follé *to you. There's something you must see.* He took hold of the bow and pulled.

I don't want to see, I said. I plunged the push pole deep into the muck and held tight, but the pole broke. The pirogue slid forward. The man kept on.

Then, in the light, another man, this one stretched flat across the water, as flat as the surface of the water itself. He might have been a reflection. The wild-haired man said, *Look, Marie.* I looked and saw the coat I had so often mended, and the broad shape of the back that had carried my children to their graves.

Who are you? I asked the wild-haired man.

N'onc Télémaque!

You aren't. Your French is terrible.

Ouais! I was lost in the cutoff years ago. His mustache twitched. The swamp's deep hush pushed closer. Darkness crowded out the lantern light. Beneath the mustache, a smile moved like a worm.

A LITTLE CHAT

I dreamt I was in my own bed. There was a man in my dream, mustached and white-haired, who was and was not Mark Twain. He reclined next to me against the pillows. We were having a chat.

The old man spoke between puffs on his pipe. "I traveled the world, met gods in India and men on islands who ate their fellow men, and having seen the world, I am certain of one thing: the bulk of mankind occupies a place somewhere between the angels," he said, "and the French."

"But we are French," I said.

"Did I say *the French,* my dear? I meant *the cannibals.*" The old man groomed his mustache with his fingers. "I'll tell you," he said, "a curious and pathetic fact of life. When your children are grown, they are not the persons they were. Those little selves have wandered away, never to return, except in dreams. They tarry a moment and gladden the eye, then vanish and break the heart." Reaching under the counterpane, he brought forth a turnip, held it out to me, mustache a-twitch. "Better to eat them while they're young."

When I came out of my faint, the pirogue was lodged among cypress knees, and the winter sun set white fire to the swamp.

ACROSS THE GREAT BAYOU

I walked for thirty miles through flooded fields that, come summer, would be shifting and silvery blue with sugarcane—which, come autumn, would fetch no price at all. I passed the huts of fellow sharecroppers, French or Negro or both. Sometimes they let me sleep in their sheds. I came upon rickety shrines built of scrap wood, and I knelt and lit votives at the altars where chipped ceramic saints congregated in memory of a dead child, in thanks for a healed child, in petition for better times. I ate bullfrogs, when I could catch them.

Then, after fields upon fields, after days and nights—a thicket of trees, just darker than the dark sky, and beyond them, at last, the River. Under no moon at all, I trampled through the tangled leafless vines and pulled off my shoes. I laid LeLe's coat over a low-hanging branch. I left my ragged dress crumpled in the mud. My body quaked with cold, my bones clattered. *But my children,* thought I, *are still colder.* I filled the jar with water, closed it tight, and left it on the bank.

Then I walked into the River. My body numbed. I floated.

Stars swirled and flashed but closely kept their light. A comet trekked across the sky. I was a dark wrinkle, a rivulet, in the greater darkness.

There was a light on the other side of the wide River, and I swam toward it. My numb body did not realize how far it swam. The light blazed steadier and brighter than any lantern. It came from the upstairs windows of a large white house, and in one of those windows a man sat writing at a desk, under an electric lamp. A pipe drooped from his lips. The smoke drifted around his tilted white head. He looked up from time to time, out the window, and I was afraid he might see me there, naked and shivering in his River. But he saw nothing. His eyes were pinched. He rocked back and forth in his chair and massaged his chest with one hand. Now and then he seemed to be gasping for air.

I watched the man for a long time, until he finally put down his pen and rose from the desk. Then the windows went black all at once.

ST. JOSEPH'S DAY

Not Mardi Gras, no orgy of chicken chasing or last fattening in a time of fatness. By St. Joseph's Day, we are all Lent-thin. For LeLe's sake, who learned the custom from her Italian mother, on this saint's-day meridian in a forty-day fast, we will pretend a break, we will pretend a feast. But we were hungry before Lent and will be hungry after Easter.

At dawn we gather around LeLe's makeshift altar (her kitchen table on any other day). We have brought what we could for St. Joseph's feast. A spoonful of preserves, a potato, a turnip, a catfish that someone pulled from the swamp, water from the River in a covered jar.

Père Alceé murmurs blessings in Latin, and Ovide Latourneau confirms them in French. LeLe's dumb child in white, the silent suffering Virgin, waits at the altar for St. Joseph to come. She points at the catfish and looks to her mother. *That's for St. Joseph,* says LeLe. LeLe thinks St. Joseph will make the child speak.

I say, *We'll see, LeLe. If St. Joseph comes.*

The other two Maries say, *He'll come, LeLe. He'll come. Hasn't he always come before?*

LeLe lights her candles and waits. All of us move closer for warmth.

The noon sun has begun to heat the kitchen when someone rattles the door. LeLe pokes her child awake and seats her at the table. The hands of the women of the parish flit about the table, arranging plates, cups, forks, and food. Père Alceé lets the visitor in.

"Bienvenue, St. Joseph!"

"Amen."

"Il est arrivé!"

The child begins to cry. She knows you. The robes and staff do not hide who you are. You sit down to table and try to make her laugh, but she will not look at your funny faces. You fork a turnip and offer it to the child.

You must thank St. Joseph for coming, LeLe scolds her.

I have poured water from the River into your cup. You reach for it and toast our parish: *"Vous-autre est le bon monde!"*

He speaks French! LeLe says.

Latourneau whispers back, *Yes, badly.*

When you sip from your cup, something changes in your face. The child wails and shrinks from the table. Before you dissolved into a heap of ash in your chair, I think you may have looked at me and winked.

I punt the pirogue into the swamp and scatter your ashes there, you snake. In my empty home, I will light a red candle upside down. I will wait for the River to flood.

Haguillory

When Haguillory woke up at four thirty and went to the kitchen in his shorts and slippers, Dot was already there at the table, tanked up on coffee. He poured himself a cup without much looking at his wife. Outside the kitchen window, his tomatoes blushed in the moonlight. The blue crabs down in the Sabine marshes would have been gorging all night under that bright full moon, and this morning Haguillory planned to go crabbing.

He fixed his coffee and pretended there was nothing strange about Dot sitting up before dawn, when she was usually in bed until nine or ten. Her joints kept her up late, and on top of that, she'd get herself all worked up watching the late-night news or reading the paper. How she could stand it, he didn't know; it was always the same thing: New Orleans this, Katrina that, like those people were the only ones who'd been hit by a storm.

In the wee hours, she would finally bump down the hall to sleep in the extra room, the one that used to be for the kids, and wake Haguillory up on the way, dropping her late-night dishes in the sink, closing doors harder than she needed to. Lord, did she make some racket moving around the house. Then she'd stay in that room, with the door shut, until long after sunrise. Maybe she was sleeping, or maybe she was sick of his face. He was sick of hers, too, most days.

Never mind, though. At least Haguillory could, in these dark morning hours, wholly inhabit the kitchen: coffeepot, preserves, dainty demitasse cups and silverware Dot saved for company. He played house in the morning dark. He even cleaned up after himself.

But it was different with her sitting there. He had learned, in his five years of retirement, that if he helped with house-work, she yelled, whereas if he left a trail of grime and dirt and crumbs as he went about his day, she rewarded him with a petulant silence. Therefore, with her at the table, he spilled some sugar onto the counter, stirred and sloshed coffee out of the cup, then left the spoon on top of the coffeemaker. For good measure, he swept the spilled sugar onto the floor.

She spoke anyway. "I'm going with you this morning. I done put some Cokes in the cooler, and I had my bath. Go put your clothes on."

"Tide don't come in till nine," he lied. Maybe she'd go back to bed.

"I want to see how things are down there."

"About the same as last time. No point looking at it again."

"How could it be the same? That was months ago." She grabbed hold of the table's edge, rocked a couple of times, and pulled herself creaking and popping out of the chair. "Let's beat the crowd," she said.

"We don't got to go *now*."

But she was already out the door.

This time of morning, the August day was an oven set to *Keep Warm*. By midmorning, they'd be back up to *Broil,* and Dot would be spitting mean—mean as a cat with its tail on fire.

Maybe she'd still change her mind, with the heat coming on like it was. Haguillory stalled for a little while in the garden, picking a few nearly ripe tomatoes and unloading a vine of dewy string beans. The lawn beyond the garden was littered with wilted leaves and pecans, still in their green husks, all fallen into his yard from the neighbor's tree, just across the property line. He gathered the pecans in a flap of untucked shirt. The moon hanging in the dark sky shone through the bare branches of the tree. It was dying, that tree, no question. Well, good.

For all old man Matherne had to know, the storm could have done that. Haguillory's own trees hadn't been the same since Rita hit last year. They were gaunt and crooked. There was sun in the yard where there used to be shade. One of the oaks had dropped its thickest limb through his roof, right over the living room. When he and Dot had come home, almost a week after the storm, he found his favorite chair soaked and growing black paisleys of mildew; it had to be put to the street, along with the end table he'd built, and the TV remote control, and his fishing magazines, and his lamp, and the vibrating pad for his back. All ruined.

On his way to the garage, Haguillory dumped the load of

pecans noisily into the garbage can. Then he loaded the nets, twine, cooler, tackle box, fishing rod, and a couple of lawn chairs onto the bed of the truck.

Dot, in the cab, had twisted her head around to watch him. She was saying something through the glass. When he opened the driver's door, she said, "I was trying to tell you to grab me a hat."

He slunk his hand behind the bench seat and pulled out the lopsided, sweat-stained straw contraption that their son, Danny, used to wear when Haguillory took him fishing, just the two of them, father and son. But they didn't do that anymore. His son didn't come around much at all—not since Haguillory spoke his mind about that child Danny and his wife adopted two years ago out of some country he'd never heard of. They already had a kid of their own. Why did they need another one? The hat was dry-rotted and raveling at the rim and too big for Dot's head, but she had the good sense to keep her mouth shut about it when he handed it over.

He had planned to pick up a package of melt at the grocery around the corner before heading south into the marsh, but after parking outside the store he saw that it didn't open until six.

"*Mais,* I could have told you that," Dot said. "We can stop in Hackberry."

"They won't have melt."

"What you think? Sulphur is the only town with melt? They have melt in Hackberry."

"I don't know if that store is still standing."

"It is. It was on the news."

Her and her news.

In the truck cab they were as close as they had been, physically speaking, in a very long time. They did not sleep in the same bed anymore. They did not eat together at the same table. They did not visit the same friends; or rather, Dot visited the same friends and Haguillory visited no one at all. She'd been especially prickly after that week of evacuation last fall at Danny's house up in DeRidder. Well, that hadn't been fun for anyone. Air mattresses on the floor. Fighting for the television or, when the power went out, for the lanterns and battery-powered fans or, days later, for the better MREs. Their daughter, Carol, with that good-for-nothing boyfriend of hers, sharing a mattress in front of everybody. And the adopted child, not quite right, with her foreign lisp and feline eyes. She was about ten, just a few years older than Danny's natural son, and you could see the little boy tense up whenever she got too close, like a dog expecting a kick. There was that screaming fit she'd thrown, with a fork in her hand, when she got the ham-slice MRE instead of the chili and macaroni. Haguillory said, so she could hear, that they ought to send her back to where she came from, if it was so bad here. The girl had to learn. Dot hadn't liked that at all. But what? Did she think he had fun saying that kind of truth?

Now here they were, in the truck, with nothing to listen to but AM radio and each other coughing, snuffling, and throat-clearing. Between Lake Charles and Hackberry, they spoke to each other only once, about a quarter of an hour into the drive. With the light coming up, they could see a storm building in the west, with a few vanguard clouds above. From time to time, the sky spat on their windshield. They drove by a pasture that held a herd of red cows.

"Look at them cows," Haguillory said. "They all in a clump. Gonna get some rain today."

Dot clucked her tongue. "Them cows are scattered."

"Aw!" said Haguillory.

The Hackberry store was indeed standing, although a third of its roof was draped in blue plastic. Across the street a house that had been neatly halved by a fallen oak tree was fronted by a FEMA trailer. The pasture next to the store had been turned into an appliance graveyard filled with row upon row of taped-up refrigerators and freezers, ruined washers, dryers and stoves. A fridge on the outer row said, in red spray-painted letters, DO NOT OPEN! INSURANCE ADJUSTER INSIDE!

Haguillory laughed.

The store, which was the last stop before you got to the oil reserve, was busy, even this early, with young men in their industrial blues getting fried chicken and pizza slices from the hot bar for their lunch. Dot waddled along beside Haguillory, then stopped, picked up a package of boudin on sale, and took out her glasses to read the label. He didn't wait for her.

A sleepy teenager manned the store's meat counter. He was wrapping up a pound of shrimp for another old man in sagging khaki coveralls and a cap. When it came his turn, Haguillory tapped the glass lid of a refrigerated unit and asked the boy how much the night crawlers were.

"What we need night crawlers for?" Dot said, pulling up next to him. "We don't need no night crawlers."

"If I want to fish!" Haguillory snapped. "How much you asking for them?"

"Two dollars," the boy said.

"Shoo! Two dollars for some worms?"

The teenager said nothing.

Haguillory hovered for a while, then finally slid the glass back and reached down to pluck one of the little Styrofoam boxes from the stack. He opened the lid and peered into the dirt. A thick pink segment of worm throbbed on the surface.

"You just looking to *lamentation*," Dot said.

"How many they got in here?" Haguillory asked.

"I don't know. A bunch." The teenager looked around for another customer.

"Two pounds of melt," Dot said, stepping past her husband like he was just some old man taking too long to make up his mind.

"No melt today."

"Aw!" said Haguillory.

"We'll get us some chicken necks instead," Dot said.

"You think the crabs don't know the difference?"

"The crabs *don't* know the difference."

It was almost full daylight when Haguillory and Dot at last got themselves established in lawn chairs on the footbridge that crossed the canal. From each of four bridge pilings they dangled chicken necks on lengths of twine. The marsh grass shivered in a little bit of a breeze. Dense, iron-blue clouds were mustering to the west, but they had a few good hours before the storm would break here. The truck was parked nearby, on the highway median, and they could get to it fast.

Every few minutes, Haguillory, restless, would get up

from his chair and take one of the lines in hand, ever so gently easing the chicken neck up from the depths of the brackish water until it appeared just below the surface. If he felt a tug or spied a dogged claw, he'd say, "Pass me that net! Quick! Quick!"

But Dot was seldom quick. Sometimes she was distracted, fussing in her purse for a hankie or for aspirin, which she was taking in handfuls, or for whatever else was in that apparently bottomless sack. But when she was quick, she was too quick, and her shadow passing suddenly over the water would send the crab skittering back into the murk.

"What, you never caught a crab before?" he said.

They had been out there a little more than two hours and had netted exactly five crabs when another car pulled in behind their truck. Before the brake lights had even gone off, a woman threw open the passenger door and charged down the gravel shoulder toward the footbridge, shaking her head and mouthing what could only be curses. Two boys, maybe eight and ten, emerged, sheepish, from the back seat and trailed after her. The smaller one wore a huge T-shirt that swallowed his shoulders and reached to his knees. They were all of them in white rubber shrimping boots many sizes too big. The driver cut the motor and opened his door. He leaned against the car, resting his crossed arms on the roof and looking after the woman and the boys. A baseball cap cut a shadow across his eyes and cheeks.

The woman stopped suddenly, turned around. She flung her arms over her head and dropped them to her sides. "Are you sure this is where?" she yelled back at the man. The man half-nodded, half-shrugged, and a frustrated growl came from the woman's chest. She set off again for the bridge. "Perkins!" she called out. "Mr. Perks!"

The boys started too—a chirping chorus of "Perkins! Perkins!"—the older one louder and more zealous.

"Lord have mercy," Haguillory said.

Dot reached into the cooler, past the clattering crabs, for an RC Cola and a root beer. "Here," she said. "Drink your root beer." She took off her shoes and wriggled her toes. She was red-faced and sweating. The church bulletin she had folded into a fan wasn't doing her much good.

The woman was now before them. The two boys clomped up the bridge in their big white boots and hung on the railing, one casting his eyes out across the marsh, the other down into the water.

"Y'all seen a cat around here?" the woman said. She looked like a shriveled little monkey, Haguillory thought, with a sharp little monkey face and angry, clasping monkey hands. Her bristly peroxide hair stood up straight and square, like a fez.

"We ain't seen no cat out here," Haguillory said.

"What does it look like?" Dot asked.

"That son of a bitch back there," the woman said, jerking her head back toward the car in the median, and the younger boy's shoulders hunched up to his ears.

That son of a bitch, presumably the boys' father, was now mounting the bridge, hands in pockets, toothpick in teeth. "Any luck?" he said, looking at no one, and he could have meant the crabs or the cat.

"He don't have any *claws,*" the woman said and stalked off, over the bridge and into the grass. "Perkins!" she yelled.

The older boy followed her and the younger one hung back, still gazing down into the water. Their father leaned against the bridge railing next to the younger boy. Behind him, the woman and the older boy were fanning out into the marsh in lurching, sloshing steps, parting the cordgrass with their hands as they went and calling the cat.

"Y'all catching any?" the man said.

"Just enough to make you mad," Haguillory said.

"Really?" the man said. "I'm surprised. The crabs been going nuts since the storm knocked out those flood weirs. Still pretty high salt, even into Sweet Lake."

"It ain't for lack of crabs," Haguillory said.

Dot cut him a pair of eyes, and he took up his fishing rod. He opened the container he'd bought at the store and tugged a night crawler out of the dirt. He pinched it in two, tossed half back in the dirt, and threaded the other half onto the hook. About three feet up the line, he attached a plastic cork, then wiped his gooey fingers on his coveralls. He scooted his chair closer to the water and dropped the line in. He'd see what else was there to be caught.

"*Mais,* what?" Dot said to the man. "You dumped her cat in the marsh?"

"He kept peeing on my bunk," the boy said quietly, then squatted, stretched the T-shirt over his knees, and tucked it under the toes of his boots. He pulled on one of the crab lines, hand over hand, as slowly as if he were creeping up on a rabbit. After a while, he reached out an arm, fluttered his fingers. "There's a big one on here. Gimme the net. I'll pull it in for you." But nobody gave him the net. "There it goes," he said, sighing.

"Y'all can't imagine what it's like," the boy's father said. "Three adults, two kids, and a incontinent cat. In a ten-by-thirty-foot box? Nobody can live like that. It's been almost a year!" He stripped off his hat and beat it against his thigh.

"*Ç'est un bonrien,* that FEMA," Haguillory said. He spat into the canal. This young fella and his family, that little boy with his shirt too big—they'd never show *that* on the news. It was sad, how they forgot about some people, not about others. He himself was still waiting on payment for the damage Rita had done to his roof. "I'm sick to death of Katrina," he said. "You don't hear about nothing else!"

He was fixing to say more—about all the people in this world, like those looters in flooded New Orleans or that little adopted girl at Danny's, who seemed to think their suffering entitled them to inflict suffering on others—when the cork on his fishing line dipped below the surface. He jerked the rod to the right, stood up from his chair, and began reeling in the line, the tip of the rod arching and quivering with the weight of whatever was down there tugging. What was down there was a little garfish, about a foot and a half long, maybe two pounds.

Haguillory grabbed it behind the gills. "Reach me those pliers," he said to Dot, and she did. "Young man," Haguillory said, "you know what that is?"

The boy came closer, eyed the fish. "That's a gar."

"That's one ugly fish," Haguillory said, and he felt the ugliness of the fish in a frisson down his spine. The eel-like body, the long jaws opening and closing, the needle teeth and staring eyes, the blood pooling around the hook in its cheek. He jerked out the bare hook; then he wrapped the pliers around the base of the gar's snout. Those night crawlers didn't come cheap. "Watch what I do with that fish," he said, and he squeezed until, with a crunch, the snout snapped off and fell to the planks at his feet. The little fish thrashed in his hand, working what was left of its jaw. Haguillory leaned over the railing and dropped the fish back into the water. He wiped his hands on his coveralls and sat. "Now," he said to the boy. "You see?"

"Yes, sir," the boy said and looked up at his father.

"Those are trash fish," the man said. He jammed his hat backward onto the boy's head and gave the brim a little tug. "I never could eat those, myself."

Dot made that noise with her tongue. *"T'a pas honte!"* she said. She got up, wobbly, and crossed the bridge, following the path to the marsh. Out there in the grass, the woman was shouting something at the older boy. Dot reached the end of the path, held out one arm for balance, and tested the mucky ground with her foot.

"You going to fall over if you try that," Haguillory said, but she didn't listen. Fine. Let her break a hip. Was it his fault the gar was an ugly fish?

He lifted his tackle box onto his lap and dug around until he found a multi-tool that he'd won as a door prize at one of the IUPAT gumbo luncheons the painters' union put on. It had pliers, a screwdriver, a knife, a toothpick: a good little tool. He never used it. He held it out to the boy. "You want that?"

The boy shrugged. "Sure," he said, and took it. The tool disappeared under his T-shirt.

"Tell the man thank you," the boy's father said.

"Thank you."

"I'm sorry for y'all," Haguillory said.

The sky had gone dark in the time since this family had arrived, the storm nearly upon them. To the west a single, stunning bolt of lightning touched the marsh, chased by a whipcrack of thunder.

The boy ducked and cringed like a little animal, then glanced at his father and smiled, embarrassed.

"We better get going," the man said. He called out to the woman and the older boy, but they were already coming back.

Dot was talking with the woman, who was moving her hands, excited. She pointed, back toward Hackberry and the direction from which they had come, then swung her finger around to the man on the bridge and jabbed the air. Dot wagged her head violently and talked for a while, too, pointing occasionally at Haguillory.

The older boy reached the bridge first.

"Well?" the man said, and the boy said nothing. He bumped the shoulder of the younger one when he passed.

Then came Dot and the woman. The woman scooped the younger boy to her side, held him against her hip. "We'll come back tomorrow," she said and eyed the lightning to the west.

The deep hum of thunder buzzed in Haguillory's chest.

"It's been a week," the man said. "That cat is probably long gone."

"Maybe if you'd said something earlier," the woman said, "instead of letting us think he ran away. And after all that."

It looked to Haguillory like she was going to cry. Over a cat.

"Y'all have no idea what we went through to keep that cat with us."

"Oh, *chère,*" Dot said.

"I'm going to leave you my phone number," the woman said. She patted herself down, like she might actually have a pen and paper stashed in those cutoffs. "Y'all have something to write with?"

"Just tell me the number," Haguillory said. "I'll remember."

"He won't remember. Here, I've got a pen in my purse." Dot dug in her purse, forever. Once the woman had the pen, there was the problem of something to write on, but Dot held out her palm. "Write it here."

The woman wrote the number and called out to the cat a few more times before turning abruptly away.

"Y'all stay dry," the man said.

The boy in the big T-shirt gave Haguillory a quick, down-at-the-hip wave. His older brother was already waiting at the car, staring down the highway, arms stiff at his sides, hands clenched into fists, like he was trying to see clear to the Gulf. The man went to him, laid a palm on the nape of his neck, steered him gently into the back seat, and shut the door. They all settled in and drove away.

"Over a cat," Haguillory said, and started to gather their things. He cut the crab lines off the pilings and let the loose ends of twine slide into the canal. He secured the hook to the rod and reeled the line in tight, then folded the chairs and propped them and the net and the rod against the cooler. A fat drop of rain tapped his arm. Another one, his neck.

Dot just stood there, watching.

Haguillory knelt down and closed his tackle box.

"You think I don't know what you did to Matherne's tree?" Dot said.

He pressed tight the lid on the container of worms. "What tree?"

"That pecan tree. You think I don't know?"

"The storm killed that tree!"

"Or to the Landrys' dog?"

"Aw!"

Dot raised a finger in the air. "The next time Carol calls, you're not going to hang up. You're going to talk. And if somebody tells you that somebody died, you know what you're going to say? You're going to tell them, 'I'm sorry to hear that.' You're not going to say, '*Mais,* so?' And," she said, shaking so hard her cheeks jiggled, "you're going to quit calling Zareena 'that girl Danny adopted.' She's your grand-daughter. You just call her 'my granddaughter' from now on. Do you hear me?"

"I don't have to do nothing," Haguillory said. He looked down at Dot's bare feet, her legs muddy to the calves. He wanted to say, *You going to get in my truck like that?* But it wasn't worth it.

"You're a spiteful man, and why?" she said. "*À la tête dure,* yeah. I should have known that from the beginning."

That part was true, he thought. She should have. From the very first time they met at the dance hall in Basile, when he told her—just for the hell of it—that his name was Herman, and for months, even after things had gone past dancing, she had called him Herman, and all his friends had gone along with it, snickering behind her back, until one day she asked a visiting cousin, "Where's Herman?" and he said, "Who?"

187

and she said, "Herman! He was just standing right here," and he said, "There isn't any Herman, you must mean Haguillory," and the jig was finally up. She should have known then. Fair warning. But she had married him anyhow.

"I've had just about enough," she said. She picked up her shoes, and nothing else, and turned toward the truck, flapping one hand at her side like she was shaking off a punch.

Inside the cooler, the crabs rattled around. When Haguillory opened the lid, three of them lifted their claws, furious, cursing God. Five crabs weren't even enough to bother with. He dumped them out on the bridge and kicked them, one by one, over the edge, into the water.

He carried the cooler and the fishing rod and the folding chairs to the truck. Dot was sitting in the cab, staring past the beads of rain sliding down the windshield, as if searching for something far down the road, the same way the boy had done. Well, what did they think they would find? He snuck up to her window and tapped on the glass to see if he could scare her. She didn't flinch.

When he went back to collect his tackle box and the last odds and ends from the bridge, he said, "Well, I'll be damned."

There was that cat. It crouched in the gravel path and mewled.

Haguillory wiped the rain from his forehead and arms. He bent over and wriggled his fingers. "Come here, you," he said.

The cat hesitated, meowed, tensed as if it was about to dart off into the marsh, and then lifted its tail in the air and came to Haguillory. It shoved its cheek against his shin.

He cast a glance over his shoulder at the truck. Dot was leaning across the seat, reaching for the key, which he'd left in the ignition. She started the engine, adjusted the air-conditioning vents, and rested her head against the window, eyes closed.

Haguillory slipped a hand under the cat's belly and lifted it, held it against his chest. It was light and limp, purring in deep, relieved breaths. All down its sides, the fur was matted in clumps, and at the base of its tail was a solid, tangled carpet of hair and grass and shit. It smelled disgusting.

"You need a bath, you," Haguillory said.

The rain was seeping through his clothes and through the cat's fur. Its thick ruff seemed to melt away; underneath was a skinny little neck. Haguillory smoothed his hand over the cat's forehead, flattened its ears back and held them.

"You had to pee on that little boy's bed?" he said.

Its big eyes stared, yellow and bright. He felt sorry for it, he really did, but in the end, wasn't it just a cat? He wrapped his fingers around a paw and pressed on the soft pads to spread the impotent toes. Then, as smooth and easy as he would throw a fishing line, Haguillory tossed out his arm and flung the cat, pinwheeling, over the rail and into the canal, thinking, as it splashed, we'll see how spiteful I am. Thinking, there's all kinds of meanness and all kinds of mercy, too.

Camera Obscura

It's the most unlikely things that get you: how he pours salt into his hand before sprinkling it pinch by pinch onto his asparagus; the way he looks up over his glasses with eyebrows arched and magnified eyes startled, perhaps, that the world is in fact right-side up; the green button-down shirt with the cuffs rolled to the elbows and the unflattering jeans and the thick white socks and the white rubber gardening shoes, none of which have been changed in the three days since you started to notice him at all and maybe longer; and the way he catches you watching him pinch salt onto his asparagus and blinks giant eyes at you with purpose, with resolve, because you did something like this two days ago when you noticed him watching you deliver your lunch tray to the dish cart, and he's caught on, and this is flirting, and he's going to give it a whirl. Not to mention, of course, certain pertinent details of your own personal life, namely, that you are, as of a year ago and admittedly with some reservation (hadn't there been some reservation?)—yes, in hindsight it seems like a grave mistake but at the time, how *had* you felt at the time?—married.

He lingers at the lunchroom table with no food or drink in front of him, and you realize of course that you've communicated your interest a little too clearly and he's lingering just for you, and after he's finally given up and left, your fellow teachers at the table say with revulsion (and with some affection, too) that he seems so "out of phase." What do you do when this ticklish absurdity masquerades as persistent, budding joy? What do you do?

You wander casually into his photography studio as you and the other teachers have been invited to do, to come and enjoy the camera obscura he's made of the room, lens-boxes in every boarded-up window and bedsheet partitions catching the light and colors like butterflies in a net. The outside is inside: shadowy, silent, upside down.

It makes unfamiliar what has become only recently familiar. For you, who are new to this fancy high school (where you teach kids with more money than you knew existed in the world), to this Western landscape, to the dry creek beds and enormous boulders (you thought they were only a myth!), far from the Louisiana town where you spent the years since your early adolescence scratching at—punching fingers through—a limited, muddy, boulderless map, for you, in this room, this new place is doubly strange. It is dizzying, this disorientation.

So you push aside a bedsheet and step through a shaft of projected light that contains in its colors the orange of a school bus, the gray-brown of late-summer grass, the fish-school shimmers of students dismissed. The photographer is leaning there, arms crossed like a museum guard.

You pester him with inane questions, growing bolder (boulder!) and clumsier by the minute. You ask how it works, the camera obscura. You ask him to show you his lens. You ask why the browning grass seems to sway so slowly, why the room feels so still, and you ask this unrelated thing that you've always wondered and been too embarrassed to ask—and he seems like the kind of man who would know, so here goes: *How come we're not upside down in mirrors?* You ask this and begin to comprehend the physics of mirrors at the very moment the words are leaving your mouth, and by the time he blinks that slow, deliberate blink and embarks upon an epic explanation, through which words and logic are applied at last to intuition, you understand completely the principles of reflection.

You find yourself crowding him into a corner and cut short your questions to kiss the strange mouth that you can't believe is the same mouth that smiles such a warm and charming smile (he does have a very nice smile, everyone agrees on that) but then snaps at a strawberry like a toad swallowing a moth, in three jerking, chomping bites. You remove the glasses from his eyes and say, in a voice like Ingrid Bergman—is it Ingrid Bergman? no, it's someone irrelevant from some movie you hate, but you're going to do it like Ingrid Bergman—so you say, *Oh darling, you had me at angle of incidence.*

★ ★ ★

Actually, you do not do—would not do—would you?—any of those last few things although you loll for an hour in bed one morning thinking them up while your husband clatters and clinks things in the kitchen and finally—how you wish he would stop, just *stop*—brings you coffee with a touch of cream, no sugar, just like you like it, and two pieces of toast, one buttered, one jammed, just like you like them. He is feeling good today.

In only a year, much has been revealed, including the presence in your husband's liver of a virus, the treatment for which is more agonizing than the disease itself, which will eventually kill him, but not now, not soon, maybe not for many years—years and years!—so why must the treatment come now, in this fumbling first year of marriage, two thousand miles from your selves as you knew them? The daily doses of poison leave him worn, desiccated, and patchy-haired. Yet he is unaccountably cheery! It is his nature, as it is the duck's to quack, the scorpion's to sting. Why now?

It was your choice to come here, for a job that you were far more excited about than the last one, mostly for the reason that it was somewhere other than Louisiana. You were always a little strange there, terrible at the rollicking *joie de vivre* that your uncles and aunts and cousins performed so easily, the bullshitting, the weekends fishing and swilling beer at river camps, the rapture with which they flung themselves—Tarzan-like on rope swings—into the water. And when you found a man (your now-husband) who was a little bit something else, but also a little bit the something you were, you hung on. He read a novel now and then. *Harper's. The New Yorker.* Remembered, and cared about, everything he read. Why not marry this man? Where were you going, anyway?

But so much must be struggled through, a lifetime of struggling—how could you not have considered the outrageous length of the life before you?—with this man whom admittedly, admittedly, you love but (well, why not say it?) who came with an array of exasperating qualities that predated the discovery of the virus and have continued unabated even now, quite disproving the indelible virtue of the gravely ill. It's the overdue credit cards and parking tickets, the exotic ingredients left to rot in the fridge or stale in the pantry, the expensive birthday-gift bicycle that was stolen before you even knew it was yours (he left it leaning, untethered, on the back porch all night), the time he forgot the window open and the cat fell three floors to the pavement and broke a leg. That the animal he would be if he were any animal—if he could *choose* to be any animal—is a duck. *You married a duck,* you think now. How could you have married a duck? And yet, you can't bear to imagine forgetting these things. You can't bear to think that one day, your memory of his face could be foggy and painless, that one day (not soon! not soon!) you may not be there to bicker with nurses, sleep in armchairs, and stroke the forehead of your ailing duck.

It's other things too. It's even the things you love (or thought you loved): all the reminders, great and small, that he comes from where you come from. His amused contempt for the singlewides you both grew up in. His mispronunciation of words and names he's seen but never heard (*DosteeYOOski,* he says, *BorGEEZ, Seven SAMyoureye*). That neither of you had—or even yet has—a passport. Has ever even seen a real-live passport. Has ever been anywhere, really, before moving west: Florida, Texas. Did that even count? The ironic (it was ironic, was it not?) mullet-and-mustache he wore when he first found you, a master's student alone in a Baton Rouge bar, besieged by an intensely cologned middle-aged contractor who had first admired your hairstyle and then, when you said no thanks, you just wanted to go back to your book (it was *Slouching Towards Bethlehem*), called you a cold-hearted bitch. Your would-be husband swooped in with his mullet-and-mustache, edged the contractor aside, said he'd just read an article in *The New Yorker* by Joan Didion, about Hemingway, whom he liked less than Didion herself. "'Goodbye to All That,'" he said. "Have you gotten to that one yet?"

He worked in the sprinkler business, had no better than a GED, but he was a reader, he said, sort of an autodidact, and at the word *autodidact* you swooned a little, didn't you? At the mess of contradictions? Don't you remember how you swooned? He had a truck and a GED and a Cajun name and a shelf full of Richard Brautigan. He knew where you were from, down to the very street, down to the very singlewide. *My cousin lived in that park,* he said. *Do you know So-and-So?* and you did, from the pool, from shimmying under the fence to catch frogs in the oxidation pond, from firing BB guns at the goats that kept the grass around the pond trimmed low. And you must have known him too then, one of the many sun-browned boys in swim trunks, on bikes and skateboards, rat tails at the base of their skulls, but neither of you remembered the other. Still, he knew where you were from and he knew what you were reading, and that was really something.

But here, away from his cousins and brothers and their boats, from the job where he'd risen to foreman, he is considerably diminished. He can't find work, hasn't much tried. He does not read anymore, has not bothered to put his own books on the shelves. In public, he defers to you, always. *She's the smarty,* he says, cheerily, to your colleagues and new friends, with their PhDs and ABDs and allergies and locally roasted coffees. *Talk to her.* But more and more, under the cheer, he means it, and you can hear he means it, even if no one else can. *Me, I'm just another coonass with webbed feet. All I do is quack. Quack quack!*

You can't say that here, you tell him. *Especially in front of.*

Can't say what where? he says. *Quack?*

Coonass. They'll think you're racist.

I can't reappropriate my own ethnic slur?

They'll think you're talking about black people. Like, you know. You hesitate, of course. You know better than to say such words.

Coon? He says. *That's ignorant. It comes from French. Connasse. Do you know what that means?*

You don't. All you know are the squirmy glances exchanged among your colleagues.

Cunt, he says. *It's French for cunt. Go ahead and check the OED. Cunt.*

Then, after letting that little gem hang in the air: *The only remotely brown person on the payroll at that school is the janitor. Maybe the Spanish teacher, but she's even bougier than you are. I don't appreciate being policed by hypocrites.*

Beyond all this, he is ill. This morning, after a period of grave dehydration and two days in the hospital hooked to pumps that filled him up again with fluids, he is almost wild with life. He wants to thank you, to do for you as you have done for him all these months, carrying him, carrying the insurance, really, that pays to treat an illness that is his own fault anyhow. (But wasn't that, too, one of the things you loved, still love? That he tried everything that could be tried? That he wasn't afraid when his cousins passed him a needle and said, *Try.*) How reluctantly, how peevishly you've done for him he hasn't noticed, or has refused to. *You a damned good woman, chère,* he says, putting it on like back home. *Shoo, but I got me a good woman!*

He brings you coffee and toast.

When later that same morning you bump into the photographer in the halls of the art annex where you've gone specifically to bump into him, you feel yourself turning quite red, and then—oh vampiric treachery (or, more concretely, your refusal to eat the lovingly toasted toast)—you feel yourself turning quite pale, and you know you are going to faint, and in fact, the floor and the ceiling change places and you come out of the faint with that face hanging upside-down over you. It's truly a troubling face.

It's the voice that's most confusing. It lumbers out like a friendly bear from a cave and says, "Just lie still until you're sure you can stand." And though he's still in that awful green shirt, he smells like sawdust and his hand is warm and enormous and sweeps the hair back from your forehead. The principal says to you, "Are you ill? Do you want a doctor?" and you say, "No doctor," and the Spanish teacher, the closest thing you have to a friend in this new place, squats down, leans in close to your ear and whispers, "Maybe you're pregnant, *chica*."

You can see the photographer has heard this too, and there is an embarrassing, unspoken implication, though if pressed you couldn't name it, and he blinks his eyes, but you fling out your arms in search of the tile, knocking away his hand, and finally you distinguish up from down and you're standing and he's still on the floor. Now, you snatch up your things. You bolt.

When you see him again at lunch, he says, "Have you recovered from your *spell*?" and you say, "I have," and while you eat you find yourself leaning slightly in, slightly toward him, and you're afraid your colleagues will notice the leaning, but lean you must, so lean you do. He crosses his legs and his rubber shoe rests lightly against your shin. You pretend to be the table.

For the next day, you celebrate, secretly. You feel you have passed a test, and you will allow yourself outrageous and wicked flights of fancy. You will pack up your things, move out on the husband, divorce, and marry immediately this brilliant, odd-looking man, and you will have brilliant, odd-looking children, and you will adore them all, and you will make them sometimes change their clothes. It will be saintly, how you adore them.

This almost, but not quite—not nearly—actually not at all assuages the guilt of even thinking of abandoning a man who will one day—not today, not tomorrow, not even soon!—be laid low by his own liver. It is amazing how often this slips your mind. You are appalled at the bifurcation of self that has allowed such thoughts. At the forgetfulness that, among other things, causes you in the middle of a grammar lesson, in front of fifteen mystified fifteen-year-olds, to laugh hysterically at the double entendre in a dangling (dangling!) modifier.

You concoct elaborate reasons to enter a room where he is, and once in that room, you panic and make abrupt, inexplicable exits. At school events you try to sit near him, not next to but directly behind, perhaps. At an assembly in the old Spanish mission that serves as a lecture hall and theater, he is in front of you, just to the right, and about fifteen minutes into the principal's tirade against uncited or fallacious internet sources, against plagiarism, against cheating, you see him gazing at the ceiling, taking mental measurements of the room, of the windows, and he turns around and says softly, "I'm going to turn this place into a camera obscura." You notice that he has changed his shirt.

For a week you see him crossing from studio to woodshop to lecture hall and back again with little wooden boxes and mirrors tucked under his arms. He boards up the windows in the lecture hall one by one. You run into him in the teacher's lounge, and in a convulsion of glee he pulls from his wallet a mail-order invoice for two dozen lenses. He rattles it at you. "By the end of the week!" he says. Over lunch, he will speak of nothing but focal lengths and apertures. In that he is speaking at all, this is a vast improvement in his social behavior, but in another sense this development is, for your colleagues, excruciating. You listen, conspicuously and intensely. To everyone's chagrin, you invite elaboration.

On Tuesday morning, between the usual announcements for quiz-bowl practice and yearbook orders, he proclaims over the intercom the unveiling of the camera obscura. After the last bell, you come in with a group of other teachers, and you all take seats and drop your heads back to see the puddles of light on the ceiling above each window. One by one the others get up, say into the darkness *This is amazing, good work there, buddy,* and exit, and you finally realize that you and he are alone in the camera obscura.

He emerges from the shadows near you and says, "I've found that the best way to experience this is to lie down." And you both lie down in the aisles and watch the clouds move across the ceiling, the leaves flutter slowly in the trees, no accompaniment to this movement but the creaking of floorboards under your back, the rush of your breath, and the electric sizzle (are you imagining this?) between your feet and his, no, that's the click and hiss of an IV drip in the stillness of a hospital room, like the steady click and hiss of a camera on time-lapse, or actually it is his camera on time-lapse and it's recording the reflected movement of clouds. On the ceiling just above you is the main road and the gas station across from the school, its empty parking lot, utter stillness, and when a blurred human form exits the gas station and moves away, toward the frayed edges of projected light, and then disappears into shadow, it's like discovering a code in the static of space. It is frightening and ominous and sad, it is a glimpse of the future of a memory.

You think: *We are watching forgetting. This is what forgetting looks like.*

You take a breath and say this, and there is no answer.

Half an hour passes and the two of you manage this much more conversation:

"Is it Tuesday?"

"Yes, it is Tuesday."

Finally, with nothing else to say, you pick yourself up from the floor, dust yourself off. You're right in front of the lens box, your head is blocking the sun—you can feel the hot coin of it on the back of your skull—and you idiotically make hand shadows of an octopus swimming across the sky. There is no response. As you shuffle up the aisle, he says from the darkness, "Thanks for coming. Come back!" and you wonder if he means right now, tomorrow, or nothing at all.

One buoyant blue morning you are inexplicably crackling like cellophane, trembling with agapē. This morning, this joy is a balloon that you tap with the tips of your fingers, a slow volley to the janitor, and he taps it back to you, and to the principal, and he taps it back to you, and to the Spanish teacher (who is now absolutely certain that you are "expecting," and you are, but what? what are you expecting?)—*tap!* with a flourish of wriggling fingers—and each of them smiles a true smile, a this-morning-in-June smile (although it is, of course, not June but nearly November).

It's the weather. It's only the effect of the weather. Such interminably, oppressively beautiful weather.

It compels you to ask the photographer if he would like, after school, to go for a hike. When you call your husband, you don't even bother to lie. He has seen the photographer (granted, from a distance, when picking you up from school), and you have composed a careful portrait besides—the rubber shoes, the off-kilter remarks. This could not be more than simply a hike.

He has a cowboy-ish walk, very straight, and he strolls over boulders with no change in his posture, never bending, never grappling for a foothold, not at all like the scrambling squirrel you are. You trip over rocks, fall on your ass not once but twice. "We don't have rocks where I come from," you say, and he laughs, but it isn't really a joke. You and he climb up and up, up and up. Finally you reach the top, the end, the vista, and there at the vista, there is a bench, only feet from a fierce drop-off.

You both sit on the bench with a little space between you. You hear him swallowing. A tumble of frivolous questions presses, but you wait. Your teeth are chattering, you are shivering, although it is easily seventy degrees. You pretend to enjoy the beautiful view.

"So," he says. "You moved here from the South. Where, again?"

"Louisiana."

"You don't have an accent."

"No," you say. "I got rid of it. Like Hilda Doolittle."

"Eliza," he says flatly. "Hilda is the poet. Eliza is the fair lady."

"Right. Whoops." Then, for no good reason, you say it again: "Whoops."

"I've never been there," he says. "Is it nice?"

You laugh. "Have you even heard of the South?" You wisecrack about racists and mullets and singlewides and meth-addict cousins in prison and when he only blinks at you, you think, okay, maybe I ought to be done making these jokes.

"You must be homesick," he says, without sarcasm.

"Never," you say. "Look at all this." You sweep a hand at the vista. You are so far from everywhere. How did you get here?

"It must be nice to be from some place. My parents moved around a lot," he says.

"Military?"

"Hippies." He laughs but only in his chest and weirdly without moving his face. "They had a good time, but it was hard on me."

You look at each other, at the same time, for the first time. He blinks and you blink. There is something yet that needs to be said.

He says, "Aren't you—?"

When the word *married* bobs to the surface like a drowned corpse, you feel like the world is upended and you will be shaken off. It's gone over the cliff, whatever it was that sat between you, you kicked it over the cliff and you can hear it whistling all the way down until it hits the bottom in a little puff of dust. You begin the funereal march back down the trail.

There is silence for the first fifteen minutes of the journey, and you wonder through this silence if there is something required of you, an apology, an abandonment of ethics, but then, suddenly, he is merciful. He breaks into song, a sea shanty. *O the year was 1778—how I wish I was in Sherbrooke now!* You think at some point he'll surely stop, but he does not stop. He knows every verse, sings the whole thing—it goes on and on—in a robust monotone all the way back down to the trailhead. Throws back his head for the final refrain and shouts it at the treetops: *Goddamn them all!*

You are in a state of vapid waiting. Your skull is a lean-to and you're camped out under it, waiting for a change in the weather. There is no change in the weather. You start to blurt cryptic things to the colleagues, to the husband. Things like: *My skull is a lean-to and I'm camping out under it.* You feel you are speaking in rebuses. You have trouble stepping outside the situation enough to determine exactly what is the problem, and exactly how much of a problem the problem is. You begin to suspect the problem is probably you.

At home, your husband resorts to antics. He requires your attention. (Of course he does. Of course he requires your attention.) He begins with little gestures, like startling kisses on the neck while you stand petrified before an open cabinet in your kitchen, arrested by despair in mid-reach for a coffee cup. Or he grabs you in a hug, pins your arms to your body, tweaks your breasts. It's playful but angry too. Finally, he throws up his hands and says, "I just don't understand."

"What?" you say.

His eyes are bloodshot. He looks dried out, almost crisp. His fingers. His ears.

"The sad," he says. "You got what you want. We came all this way. I just don't understand the fucking sad."

You decide to come clean. You will take your chances with your one friend, the Spanish teacher. A unicorn, she appears only to virgins, the pure of heart. Her eyes are wide and dewy, her gait is graceful, rolling—where her hips go, the rest of her follows. She grew up in Portland, the child of a social-science professor and a reiki therapist. She told you once that she has exceptional—even mystical—powers of empathy, and you, earthbound flesh, believed her. You are beginning to know better, but all the same she is a friend, your only friend, and the least discreet in her eye-rolling at your husband's many social faux pas, so you confide everything—the virus, the camera obscura—but when you do, she cringes, as if you have raised your hand to strike her, and you think, *My God, is it so awful, my God, is* this *my nature?* She says, "Your husband is sick. Why are you doing this?"

"But I didn't," you say, "I didn't *do* anything."

As for the unicorn, she will appear to you no more. But screw the unicorns, you think, let's be more objective. The fact *is,* before all this, before the obligating virus, you had been thinking that you'd better just pick someone to love already and be done with it. Love, you told yourself, after two critical, devastating failures, is a choice and not a visitation, is not the shared transport of a 4:00 a.m. binge on Borges (as in *BORhehs*) and a can of sardines, is not transcendence or revelation, has no empirical epistemology. It is like-mindedness on questions of dinner and dishes and laundry. It is, you have learned now, tolerance of peculiar sounds from the bathroom, the daily jamming of needles into thighs. You pick someone, that's all. You pick someone who knows where you are from and dig in. Ritual evokes reverence; every injection, every slice of buttered toast conjures affection. Was this cynicism or was it faith?

★   ★   ★

At home, your husband has excused himself from living. Your health insurance is the only thing between him and—what, exactly? This is also unclear. He plays video games. He has drawn the living-room curtains and sits cross-legged on the floor, his hands working the controller, in darkness except for the glow of the television, and surrounded by plates of shriveled pizza, crumpled taco wrappers, empty or half-full bottles of sports drink, all toppled and scattered. He spends an hour (an hour!) on the phone every day with his brother. When you ask him how he is feeling, he says, cheerily, "Fine, fine! And how are you doing?" then goes back to his game, his phone call. You might as well be greeting each other over cantaloupes at the supermarket.

Then, one evening, in who knows what season, after who knows how long, you find him there on the floor and say, "Why don't you just go home? I'll buy the ticket. Please just go home!"

"Don't yell at me," he says.

"Goddamn," he says.

"Fuck this," he says. "I thought if we left you'd be different."

As one does in times of trial, when the truth is clear except to the self, you have a dream. In your dream, your husband is a plate of sushi. He is laid out in fleshy pinks and whites upon a bed of rice and wrapped up neatly in cellophane. You peel back the cellophane—a naked, private, alarming sound—and pat the shrimp. "I'm sorry," you say. "I'm sorry this is so hard."

At school, the photographer doesn't blink at you anymore,

207

and in fact each of you pointedly ignores the other, but sometimes you still manage intentionally accidental contact. One day, you have somehow both landed on a park bench in the courtyard outside the annex. He is, incongruently, the sponsor of the school yearbook, and three art girls dash over and flutter around him, they want the key to the darkroom, and they cram themselves onto the bench, shoving the two of you together. They tug and nip at him like puppies at an old hound dog. "Oh, Mr. So-and-So, you know you can trust us!" There is gray at his temples, and—you see that you were wrong, he is actually quite handsome. How could you have been so wrong? He produces the key and the art girls dash away again, leaving you thigh to thigh on the bench.

You say—you try to say—what can you say? You say nothing.

He says nothing.

Neither of you says anything.

When the fifth-period bell goes off, you rise together, and in the confusion of walking away, out of a habit that was never actual but only imagined, you grab hands, you enfold fingers, you squeeze.

This startles both of you. It will never happen again.

The Boucherie

Of course it would be exaggerating to say that Slug had so estranged himself from the neighborhood that a phone call from him was as astonishing to Della as, say, a rainfall of fish, or blood, or manna, and as baffling in portent. Still, as Della stood phone in hand, about to wake her husband, Alvin, who was sleeping through the six o'clock news in his recliner, she sensed with a sort of holy clearness of heart that what was happening on the television—two cows dropping down through the trees and onto somebody's picnic in the park—was tied, figuratively if not causally, to the call from Slug. "*Mais,* the cows done flew," she thought.

The anchorwoman for the Baton Rouge news announced that a livestock trailer carrying over a hundred head of cattle on their way to processing had plunged over the entrance ramp railing at the Interstate 10-110 junction that morning. The driver had been speeding, possibly drunk, definitely decapitated. More than a dozen of the cattle were crushed outright. Several others survived the wreck only to climb over the edge of I-110 and drop to their deaths in the park below, while the remaining seventy or so, dazed and frightened, fled down the interstate or into the leafy shelter of the surrounding neighborhoods, followed by a band of cowboys called in for the impromptu roundup.

Fifty-three of the seventy cows had been recovered already, and all carcasses promptly removed from the roadway in time for the evening rush. Calls were still coming in, however: from kids who had a cow tied with cable to a signpost on their street; from riverboat gamblers who saw a small herd grazing on the levee downtown; from a state representative who stepped in a patty on the lawn of the Capitol. The search would continue into the night.

It was not the first time an 18-wheeler had gone over that railing, Della remembered. Back in the late seventies, absurd but true, some poor woman driving northbound on I-110 was killed when 40,000 pounds of frozen catfish dropped onto her Volkswagen. Della thought then, as she did now, that it was certainly a shame to lose all that meat, with so many people starving in this world.

When Alvin finally snorted himself awake, he first tried to make sense of the man on horseback in a cowboy costume, waving a lasso at a boxy red shorthorn under the statue of Huey Long—another advertising bid for Texas gamblers?—before he noticed his wife in the doorway, waving the phone and hissing, *"C'est Slug! C'est Slug!"* Alvin yanked the lever on his recliner, sending the footrest down with an echoing concussion that catapulted him up and out. *"C'est Slug?"* he said.

The name dropped out of his mouth in the Cajun-French way, with a drawn-out *uuhh*. "Let me talk to him."

Della held the telephone out, covering the mouthpiece with her palm. "Poor thing, you can't hardly understand what he says." She rushed to a notepad on the coffee table and scribbled Slug's name under the names of her four children and five grandchildren, all scattered to the ends of the earth. Next to Slug's she wrote: *Visit, cook, clean?* Tomorrow, in a quiet moment, the list of names on the notepad would be passed to Pearl, then from Pearl to Estelle, from Estelle to Barbara, and on down the telephone prayer line.

Alvin squinted at her and leaned into the phone. *"Quoi?"* he said quietly. *"Ain?"* he said gently. *"Ain?... Ain?... Quoi t'as dit?"*

Della thought regretfully of how foolish Slug's wife, Camille, had been. A doctor had told Camille she needed to watch her cholesterol, so she cut all meat but chicken from their diet, and would not at all countenance an egg. They stopped visiting their neighbors, terrified of the gumbos and étouffées that threatened their blood at every house. At church each Sunday for two years, the neighborhood watched Camille grow thin and papery, painted with watercolor bruises, and when finally she died of pneumonia, no one wondered why. Many now attributed Slug's present condition to the two years he'd been deprived of meat's vital nourishment. Why else would the removal of a tiny melanoma turn into an infection that, having started at such a small place by Slug's ear, now crept fast over his face like mold on bread? It was so simple. Why couldn't the doctors see?

"Ain?" Alvin said. *"Une vache?"*

Alvin wasn't much of a carpenter; measurements bored him, and he didn't have the tools or the fascination with things intricately wooden. While a gibbet did not have to be intricate, only sturdy and built to fit inside his fourteen-by-twenty-foot garage, Alvin could not even vouch for that. But Claude, down the block, could do amazing things with wood. He made reclining porch swings out of cypress that never rotted. He whittled his own fishing lures. Many years ago Claude had helped Alvin right a fallen chicken coop in exchange for a dinner of the last pullet left alive.

Because Alvin could not build, he butchered, and he was not so sure, despite what his wife said, that the stink of guts and mess of feathers, or the old ways of village barter were at all worse than the mad relay at the Winn-Dixie on senior-discount days: he and Della in separate lines, each with the limit—two nine-cents-a-pound turkeys—then the dash for the car, turkeys into the trunk, and right back for two more each at different registers before some faster senior citizen in one of those go-carts snatched them all up. These cheap and plentiful turkeys provoked his wife's instinct to hoard. In three deep freezers, Della had turkeys for the next five years' holidays, and they were not to be traded, these hard-earned birds. At the same time, she fussed, she threatened: no more live chickens, no more rabbits, no more pigeons, doves, squirrels in traps. She griped that she would never live to see the end of this meat.

Around the neighborhood, though, Alvin's garage butchery was held in the highest esteem, so for Alvin's promise of a fresh brisket and sweetbreads, Claude traded wood-working consultation, even at this late hour. He took one look at Alvin's paper-towel blueprint and smeared on a few changes with a leaky pen. "That's how they do for deer," he explained. "But deers aren't near as heavy."

"Us, we used to do it from a tree," Alvin said.

"Us too," Claude said. "We from the same place, you know. Or you forgot that?"

Claude, like Alvin, was from one of the prairie towns in Evangeline Parish, just north of Lafayette. They had come to Baton Rouge after the war, as young men, newly married, to find work in petrochemicals and construction. Claude thought Alvin had gotten uppity, though, as he ascended the ranks to plant manager, while Claude, a master carpenter but ornery and taciturn, antagonized one construction outfit after another until he finally hit retirement.

He traced over Alvin's lines until the paper towel split into a fuzzy stencil of an A-frame, deliberating aloud over weight limits and angles, then he drafted his own design on the back of a receipt from his wallet. To the basic frame, he added a crossbar with two hooks. He attached the crossbar to a block and tackle that could be tied to a truck, in case the bare strength of all the neighborhood's aging men wasn't enough. He even drew the truck.

He was dying to ask, Alvin could tell. "You got him tied in your yard right now?"

"Aw no, man," Alvin said. "He went in those Indians' yard. Slug says we better come get him quick before that little lady gets scared and calls the cops."

"He's a peculiar fella, Slug."

"Aw yeah, he is."

A moment of silent contemplation passed in observance of Slug's peculiarities. It had been a long, long time since anyone had seen Slug up close. It had been a long, long time since Slug had participated in the give-and-take.

The Indians were actually from Sudan, and had been living in the house next to Slug's for three years now. Through the mail carrier, Della stayed informed about them and their funny ways. There was a mother named Fatima, a little girl, another littler girl, and the oldest, a boy. Their last name was Nasraddin. They sometimes got packages of meat, frozen over dry ice and labeled PERISHABLE, from Halal Meats Wholesale, through overnight mail. There had been no sign of a father, but they had twice received official-looking letters from Sudan. Wasn't Sudan, Della guessed, a part of India? She never thought to look it up.

When the Sudanese family first moved in, the woman and the three children, on their own, the neighborhood watched from windows and porches. After hauling each heavy piece of furniture from truck to house, the mother and son, both so small and narrow, stood panting in the driveway while the little girls picked at acorns on the ground. The neighborhood watched them survey the remaining pieces for the next-lightest, putting off the inevitable six-foot hideaway sofa, bulky and impossible as a bull. The bright flowered shawl wrapped around the woman's head was wet with sweat, and kept sliding off. When Alvin and a few other men offered to help, the woman waved them away. She and her children climbed into the truck and surrounded the sofa. They pushed. "Not heavy," she said. The sofa shifted slightly toward the loading ramp. Her shawl slipped off again, but this time she untied it and draped it over her shoulders, like

214

an athlete drapes a towel, and said, "Thank you." The men, so oxlike and unsmiling, might have seemed presumptuous, a little crude, even threatening perhaps, advancing uninvited onto her lawn, but still Alvin thought it was a shame she didn't have someone to help her get along in a strange place, tiny as she was, with three kids.

For months, the neighborhood watched as the woman came and went at odd hours in the familiar uniforms of food service and checkout counters, with her long hair pulled tight into a bun at the back of her neck. When they sometimes found her at the end of a line, bagging their turkeys and toilet paper or wrapping their hamburgers, the people of the neighborhood wanted to say something to her, if not *Welcome,* then *Hello,* maybe, or *What do you need?* But she would thank them and look away before they had decided, and then they would doubt that it was her at all, but perhaps one of the many other dark people whose faces under fleeting scrutiny looked, quite frankly, alike.

The neighborhood watched when, a year later, the mother and son stood again on the lawn, this time with a garden hose and scrub brushes, washing splattered eggs off their windows and bricks. Much to the neighborhood's surprise, Slug emerged from his hermitage next door to cut down the deer hide that was strung like a lynching from the low branches of the Nasraddins' oak tree. News of a bombing in a government building had goaded the restless college and high school boys, who, for love of country and trouble, patrolled these neighborhoods in their pickups, rattling windows with speakers bigger than their engines. Fatima's boy, for days afterward, lurked on the front porch with a baseball bat, or lingered at the gate. He silently dared the white faces in every passing car, and when no one took his dare, he battered the knobby, exposed roots of the oak tree instead.

By the end of the second year, the neighborhood had accepted the Sudanese in that they had lost interest in the family altogether. From time to time, Della still sent a prayer around for the woman Fatima and her three children. She knew the name *Fatima* only as the holy site of Virginal apparitions somewhere off in Europe—Italy or France, maybe. To Della, that a brown woman could be so named was another sign that all the world's people more or less worshipped the same God. When she called Claude's wife, Pearl, to deliver the prayer list, Della said, "They just like us, them Indians. They love Mary and Jesus, same as us." Pearl said, almost as ornery as her husband, "I don't think they're the same."

Last year, when Alvin slaughtered the last of his rabbits, Della put in a busy morning of head smashing and fur scraping, then sent him around the neighborhood, a gut-reeking summer Santa with a bag full of carcasses and orders to visit the Indians. Alvin knocked at Slug's door first, encouraged by the blue television light flashing on the curtains. A shadow moved across the room and he knocked again. He waited, knocked, prepared himself for the shock of Slug's disfigured face should the door finally open, but it never opened.

When he rang the bell at the Nasraddin house, all at once he heard many bare feet running on linoleum. A dense uneasiness pressed on the door from the inside, but here too the door stayed shut. Alvin thought maybe he could just leave a rabbit on the front steps, and as he was fishing in the bag for a nice big one, the chain clattered, the door opened.

The woman Fatima, swathed in a purple cloth that dragged the floor, said, "You are bleeding?"

There were spatters of blood on Alvin's coveralls and, though he'd washed his hands, red on his elbows. "No, ma'am. I brought you a rabbit."

Fatima shook her head. She smiled and waved him inside her house. The shy little girls, eyes wide and wet, peeked around her purple cloth.

"I raise rabbits. Me and my wife, we can't use them all," Alvin tried. "So I give them away."

Behind his mother, the boy, about thirteen by then, leaned against the wall dressed in tight yellow sweatpants and a red T-shirt. He had grown since Alvin had first seen him out on the lawn shoving hopelessly at furniture. His shoulders were wide, his chest thick. He was almost as tall as any man. When he translated for Alvin, his voice was a boy's voice but with an oscillating croak. He grinned a wicked grin, then said to his little sisters, "Do you want a bunny?"

"No, no," Fatima said, and shook her head so vigorously that long fuzzy hair exploded out of its bun. She blurted something at her son, but he only smirked. "No," she said to Alvin.

"It's cleaned and skinned. Fresh," Alvin said.

He reached into his bag again, yearning to prove they were pretty rabbits, but Fatima swung her purple cloth around and scurried to the kitchen. The two big-eyed girls were marooned; they drew closer together.

"She says we can't eat that meat. That's what she said." The boy's English bubbled and flowed, smoother and more proper than Alvin's.

"It's clean," Alvin said. "Y'all don't eat meat, maybe?"

217

"We eat meat," the boy said. His eyes took in and then avoided the blood on Alvin's coveralls. "That's what she said to tell you."

Alvin was deciding whether or not he should be offended when Fatima returned, her purple cloth pinched into a sack in front of her. "Thank you," she said. She jutted her chin at Alvin's bag. "Open," she said. He did. She stood over it and let the cloth drop, dumping several pounds of candy over rabbit meat. "Thank you," she said.

"Thank you," Alvin said.

"Sorry. We cannot eat this meat," she said. "Stay for tea?"

Backing toward the door, Alvin said, "I got to go give these rabbits away."

"Come for tea."

"Thank you."

"Tell your wife," Fatima said, smiling, thanking, waving, closing the door.

Alvin stopped on the sidewalk and dug a caramel out of the bag. He unwrapped it thoughtfully, popped it into his mouth and continued down the block, wondering what in the world people eat, if not meat.

All the way to Slug's, flashlights in hand, Alvin and Claude scoped a route to Alvin's garage that would avoid attention. They met no one on their two-block trek. One or the other of them knew almost every resident within a four-block radius, many of whom would be invited to share in this lucky blessing from the Lord, but it was the passers-through, like the students from the college, who might make trouble, or the policeman, a neighbor's grandson, who rolled down the block every now and then to check on the old folks.

Claude and Alvin turned the flashlights off near the Nas-raddin house and paused at the chain-link gate to look and listen. Light from Fatima's windows overflowed the curtains and pooled in a narrow moat around the brick walls. Alvin clicked on his flashlight and made a quick sweep of the yard, but the beam only fell upon a droopy fig tree and a rusted barbecue pit.

The sound of an opening door sent Claude and Alvin ducking to the ground. "Y'all signaling planes out here?" The voice was familiar, if garbled.

Alvin shined the beam on Slug's porch where Slug stood, one hand holding him up against a column and the other lingering self-consciously near his chin. Only one eye, the left, reflected back under one silvered, bristling eyebrow. Half of Slug's head, from brow down to chin and back over an ear, was taped up in brownish bandages, and Alvin thought of the cartoons he'd watched with his grandchildren: the sweating pink pig who dabbed with a handkerchief and wiped his face right off, then thrashed around, grabbed blindly, a bewildered pink blank until the cartoonist leaned in with a giant pencil and gave the pig back to the world.

"You looking good, Slug. You feel good?"

"Cher Bon Dieu," Claude said.

Slug pulled down one corner of his mouth to straighten it out. "I feel all right. Can't do nothing 'bout it anyway." The words melted, dribbled down the steep slope of his mouth and drained out.

Slug's front room was tidy, tidier than Alvin expected

considering how long the man had been hiding out with no company except his son, who drove two hours every other weekend from Alexandria to haul his father to specialists in New Orleans, another hour away. But the house did not feel clean. Dust coated the furniture, evidence of a life in stasis, like gangrene in an occluded limb. Slug's house had always been neat, thanks to his fastidious wife, but a fishing magazine might be left here, or an empty glass there. Alvin saw nothing to indicate that Slug did more than mope from room to room, or sit contemplative, or brooding, or resentful, in his armchair. There was a sour-and-bitter odor hanging around Slug, of clothes left too long in the washing machine then scorched in the dryer. Alvin noticed wetness on the bulge of bandages over his ear. He tried to focus on Slug's speckled blue eye, yolk-yellow all around like a crushed robin's egg. "You doing everything them doctors tell you to?"

"*Ça connaisse pas rien,* those fool doctors." Slug's look dared Alvin or Claude to say otherwise.

"Okay," Alvin said. Slug would know about doctors.

"Y'all want that cow or not? She's in those Indians' backyard," Slug slurred. "The boy didn't see her and he shut the gate." On the way to the back door, Slug tied a lasso out of a ten-foot rope that was waiting on the kitchen table. When Claude turned on his flashlight, Slug swatted at it, nearly knocked it out of his hand. "You gonna scare that little lady," he said.

The men crossed Slug's dark, tangled lawn with their flashlights off. Something wild and quick jetted back to its den in the hedgerow at the rear end of Slug's property, and in answer, from beyond Fatima's chain-link fence, came a snort. Alvin felt the heavy presence of the animal all of a sudden. It was startling and near—all the more real for being unseen. He remembered: cows have horns, hooves, heads, tails, and they are so damned big. Ever so slowly, a very large and pale silhouette developed against the darkness like a photo negative. Grabbing up a wad of grass, Slug clucked and cooed, and the silhouette trudged closer. The big white head swung up and took the grass from Slug's open hand. He rubbed the wide space between her eyes, pinpointed one spot with his thumb, just right of center. The cow shook her head and puffed out a wet breath.

Each holding a handful of grass, the three men edged down the fence toward the gate, and the cow followed. The lights in the Nasraddin house were still on, and shadows moved against the curtains, the two little girls jumping on the sofa. Once the men were nearer the gate, Slug widened the lasso and slipped it around the cow's neck. Alvin lifted the gate latch, but the gate hung badly on its hinges and as Alvin dragged it open, it scraped against the driveway. The cow stomped her feet. Slug bent his knees and held on to the end of the slack rope as the cow backed away. Alvin could see only the blank side of Slug's face, impassive as the moon. The rope tightened.

"Grab it!" Claude yelled.

The cow swung her head from side to side. Pulling against them, she let out a loud and awful *moo*. The little girls in the house stopped jumping and poked their heads between the curtains. The men dropped the rope. The cow retreated to the backyard.

With her boy behind her, Fatima stepped out of her front

door waving a baseball bat. "Who's that?" she said. "I will call the police!"

Alvin turned a flashlight on his own face. "It's Alvin Guilbeau." He presented himself to her in the light of the open door. "You got a surprise in your backyard."

She let the bat drop to her side and said something in her language to the boy, who then disappeared into the house. Tonight, instead of a long sheet, she wore blue jeans and a dark tank top, with a turquoise shawl wrapped around her shoulders. Her feet were bare. In the air, Alvin smelled spices he'd never heard names for and remembered, for the first time in many years, the Indian markets he'd seen during the War, the cyclone of dark people in bright colors.

"*Chère,* you seen the news report tonight? You got one of them cows in your backyard," Alvin said. Fatima shook her head slightly. "A cow," Alvin said. He gestured at the back-yard. There was, to Alvin, a shroud about the faces of people who spoke languages other than his. Even when silent, they wore a vagueness about the eyes; their body language spoke in impossible accents. "Cow," Alvin said again. "Cow. Cow."

Fatima readjusted her shawl and seemed to teeter be-tween frustration and understanding. When Slug and Claude rounded the corner, tempting the animal with grass and leading it by the rope, all at once the vagueness lifted from Fatima. With the baseball bat swinging by her hip like a billy club, she swaggered down her front steps. The little girls watched from the window.

"I saw on the television!" she said.

"That's right."

"Khalid!"

222

The boy appeared again, his arms crossed over his chest, trying very hard to fill his doorway, to be the man of his doorway. "She wants you to have some tea." His voice had entirely changed. Alvin and Fatima both pointed at once, and the boy gasped.

"We should call the police?"

Fatima walked right up to the animal and scratched the thatch of hair between its ears. She motioned her boy over. Alvin watched the mother and son as they patted the cow's haunches and wondered if the Nasraddins could be trusted.

"I don't think we should call the police," Alvin said, "tonight. Let's wait and see."

"What should we wait to see?" the boy said. He glared at Alvin, bewildered or outraged.

Fatima made pensive birdlike noises between her lips. She said, "All right. Let's close the gate. It can stay in the yard. We'll call in the morning."

"No, ma'am," Alvin said. "We need to take it to my garage."

Slug emerged from the shadows. He tugged at his mouth. "Ma'am," he said, "Miss Fatima, one cow is a lot of meat."

"Mais, quoi tu fais, couillon?" Claude said. He knocked Slug with his elbow.

The boy yelped. "You're going to eat this cow?"

"Y'all welcome to some of it," Alvin said.

The boy bubbled over with urgent talking, flung his hands around, pressed closer and closer to his mother, then trailed off into English. "They're crazy!" he said to her. "They want to eat it!"

Fatima laughed, and even her laugh rippled with foreignness; Alvin could not translate it. "If you want to share," she

223

said, "my son would have to kill her with a knife." The boy seemed both astonished and very embarrassed. She patted his arm. "Khalid is a big boy," she said.

In the humans' confused silence, the cow tore at grass and swished her tail.

Fatima poked the bandage around Slug's ear not so gently with three fingers. "You need to change this," she said.

"Maybe so, yeah."

"You're not listening to the doctor." She addressed Alvin next. "Will you come tomorrow for tea? Will you bring your wife?"

Before he meant to, he said, "Yes, ma'am."

Fatima turned back to her house. Khalid started to follow, but Fatima threw out the baseball bat to stop him. "Help them, Khalid," she said. She gave him the bat, and went in to her little girls.

The boy walked along the animal's right shoulder and stroked her swaying neck. Her hooves thudded on the grass, clopped on the pavement as they passed through yards, across driveways, and behind houses. On the cow's left side, Slug and Claude each sulked in his own way, for his own reasons, as Alvin walked ahead, leading the cow by the rope and listening for cars.

"You got your daddy over there in India?" Claude said.

The boy didn't answer.

"Ain't none of your business," Slug said.

In one backyard, the cow took control of the men. She dragged them over to a garden of mustard greens and devoured half of a row before haunch-swatting and rope-tugging finally coaxed her on. The boy dropped far behind. He took swings with the bat, at dirt, trees, and telephone poles.

"I got to see India," Alvin said. "During the War. They let the cows roam the streets."

"I seen on TV," Claude said, "how they make the women walk behind the men."

"I don't know about that, but I seen the cows for myself." Alvin looked around for the boy.

"I'm telling you, they don't even let them show their faces, those women." Claude wouldn't let up.

"We aren't from India," Khalid shouted from the darkness behind them. "We're from Sudan!"

By the time they came to Alvin's house, the boy had disappeared. They led the cow into the garage and tied her to one of the beams overhead. She lifted her tail and dumped a heap onto the concrete floor. With a shovel that he took down from the rafters where it balanced along with rakes and fishing poles, Alvin scooped the crap into a paper bag so that he could use it later to fertilize the muscadine vines that crawled up a lattice at the back of the garage.

"She's crazy," Claude said. "We ain't gonna let a boy kill that cow."

"Aw, she was pulling our leg," Alvin said. "Don't get all worked up."

"You don't know what she's joking about or not. I wouldn't be surprised if she was dialing 9-1-1 right now."

"Bouche ta gueule! She won't call no cops!" Slug was at the garage door, his one eye peeping through a crack for any sight of the boy. "You know that little lady," he whispered, "she went to school for law in her country."

225

"Is that right?" Alvin said.

"And her husband. He was some kind of politician. They didn't like what he had to say over there. They shot him dead."

"Aw, no."

"So don't you ask that boy about his daddy no more."

Slug slipped out of the garage, into the darkness, and crept homeward like a possum, along walls and fences and hedges.

Della, in bed and asleep by eight o'clock, long before Alvin came in, and awake again at dawn, long before Alvin awoke, had no idea when she went out to the deep freezers in her housedress and slippers for a package of boudin to boil for breakfast that she would find a cow in her garage. When she saw it there, smelling like a circus and totally composed, she turned immediately back toward the house and just as she opened her mouth to yell, Alvin rounded the corner, still in his pajamas.

He started at her in French before she could argue. He told her about Slug and the Sudanese, and he made her see that it would be just like at Pepère's farm on autumn Saturdays, when their children were still babies. God knew what He was doing, sending that trailer truck flying in November instead of July. The flies had slacked off. The air was light and thin—perfect weather for slaughter. The neighbors would come and ask for this or that part, the brisket, the ribs, the sweetbreads or the brains, and there would be no fights about it, only merry hacking and sawing and yanking at skin. She would stuff her red sausages. Pearl would make liver gravy. Inside, their house would be close, wet with the boiling of sausages and the heat of a crowd sweating from homemade wine. "Besides," he said, "if we don't slaughter it ourselves, they just going to haul it off, cut it up, and send it right back to us at three dollars a pound. That cow came to us. She's ours." He made it sound like a good idea.

By noon, thanks to Della and the Catholic sisters of the prayer line, word got around that God had delivered unto the neighborhood a fat, unblemished cow, and they planned, sure enough, to eat it. Although some of the ladies had concerns, they had to admit the price of beef *had* gone up, and their little bit of Social Security certainly did not allow for steak and brisket every night of the week, and furthermore, if so-and-so down the block was in for a piece of the cow, then they should be too.

Della passed along all her prayers, for Slug, for her children and her grandchildren, who never called or wrote or prayed for themselves, and for Fatima, her little ones, and that angry young man of hers. "And pray," she said finally, "pray tonight we don't get caught."

It took little for Alvin to persuade Della to visit Fatima with him in the very early afternoon. Della did her hair and powdered her face, Alvin tucked in his shirt. They found a jar of fig preserves in the back of a cabinet, dusted it off, and wondered if the Nasraddins would say they could not eat figs.

The boy answered the door, slouching in his jeans and sweatshirt. He said nothing, only stepped aside to let them in. The little girls played dominoes on the carpet. The littler one said hi. She looked like she wanted to say more, but the bigger one shushed her and started to pick up the dominoes.

The boy led them into a tiny green kitchen, where Fatima stood before the stove stirring milk in a saucepan.

Fatima smiled. Della and Alvin smiled back. "Sit down," Fatima said, and gestured to the kitchen table. Della and Alvin sat.

"Your house is very nice," Della said. She searched the walls and countertops for anything unique to a Sudanese woman's kitchen, but saw only the usual things: clock, pot holder, sugar bowl, flyswatter. Della wondered what strange foods had been cooked on that stove and stored in that refrigerator. She wondered especially what might be in the freezer.

"Do y'all like figs?" She had been holding the preserves all along.

"What is figs?"

Della held up the jar for Fatima to see.

"Yes," she said. "Thank you." She said something to the boy in her language, and he went to the pantry and took out some bread. Meanwhile, an itch grew in Della to talk about the cow, cows, any cow; it seemed frivolous to talk about anything else.

"We weren't sure if y'all could eat figs," Alvin said.

"Just meat sometimes we can't eat," the boy said.

"You can eat beef?" Della asked.

"Sometimes." The boy started to leave the kitchen, but his mother spoke again, and he sat down at the table across from Della and Alvin.

Fatima set four cups and saucers on the counter. To Della's surprise, five ordinary little tea flags dangled by strings from the lip of the saucepan from which Fatima poured. Fatima served the tea, then sat down next to her son. She smiled at her guests and sipped from her cup. They smiled back and sipped from theirs. The boy kept adding sugar to his. He frowned and sighed.

"My father had cattle in Sudan," Fatima said.

"Is that right?" Alvin said. "For milk?"

"Some for milk, some for eating."

"You were blessed," Della said. "All those people starving." She did not know for sure if there were people starving in Sudan, but she thought it was a good guess. "When I was a little girl, we didn't have nothing for a long time. No cows. No chickens. Nothing. That was the Depression."

"No, ma'am," Alvin said, "we didn't have much."

Della held the cup close to her mouth and blew at the surface of the tea, wrinkling the milk skin, which she then dabbed with a forefinger, lifted out of the cup, and deposited on her saucer. Fatima graciously handed her a napkin.

"We wish you and your children would join us tonight," Alvin said. "There's going to be plenty." He sounded to Della like the door-to-door peddlers of peculiar religions who would show up every spring to invite them to revivals.

Fatima looked to her son, who had not drunk his tea but was staring down into it. "You see?" she said.

"I thought you were joking."

"He's a good boy," she said, "but he doesn't remember Sudan."

The boy pushed his chair away from the table and left the kitchen. A moment later, a door slammed somewhere in the house.

As best she could, Fatima explained about meat, what Muslims could and could not eat, and also about something she called *ummah*. She kept using that word to describe the people among whom she now lived, and this word sounded more lovely—and, because of its newness to their ears, more important—than the words they might have used to describe themselves and their gentle loyalty to each other. Behind her halting English was a persuasive warmth and insistence, a tenor that made every word seem lawful and good. She *had* been a lawyer, Della could see, and what a shame, she thought, that in this great country such a gifted woman had to wrap hamburgers.

In the *World Book Encyclopedia,* copyright 1955, that they'd bought for the children, volume by volume per ten-dollar purchase from the grocery store, Alvin read that Sudan is the largest of all African countries, and its capital, a town called Khartoum, sits on the banks of the Nile like Baton Rouge sits on the Mississippi. There is a North and there is a South. The North has cities and deserts. The South has swamps and mosquitoes, and months of nothing but rain. These people are poor. Poor, poor. Some parts of the year they starve, even though certain tribes hoard millions of cattle, sheep, goats, and camels, for social prestige, and because there just aren't enough trucks to haul them anywhere.

The name *Sudan* comes from the Arabic expression *bilad as-Sudan,* "Land of the Blacks," which seemed to Alvin to mean that the Sudanese are as likely to look like your run-of-the-mill black person down at the Walmart as they are to look Indian, that is, from-India Indian. They are Muslim. There are some Christians, in the South, who have been Christians longer than the French have been Christians, longer than the French have been *French*. How about *that*? There are some who believe in spirits, water spirits, tree spirits. The Muslims are moving in on them. When boys become men in Sudan, Alvin read, when they kill an enemy, their backs and arms and faces are cut in stripes of scars. A picture showed a young man in a white gown and turban with three dark hash marks across his cheeks. *Cicatrization,* it was called. *Ci-ca-tri-za-tion.*

Alvin's eyes gave out just before the section on the history of ancient Nubia. He closed the encyclopedia, he closed his eyes, and saw Fatima and her little girls with distended naked bellies, propped up by walking sticks. Sand spun around them like sleet. Or maybe there was no sand. Maybe their bare feet were sinking into an island of mud and swamp grass. Mosquitoes and deerflies swirled around them like slow sand. They were part of a circle of many people, Arabs and Africans and some lean-looking and dusty white people. In the center of the circle, a black man, shriveled, desiccated—by sand or by mosquitoes—held Fatima's boy by the shoulders. The boy, Khalid, faced his mother and sisters. Alvin saw Khalid's wide back bisected by the skinny and dark line of the old black man. The man withdrew a straight-bladed knife from the tool-belt thong that hung cockeyed on his hips. One smooth stroke across Khalid's shoulders, and blood swelled and overflowed. While the circle of men and women and children hooted and laughed and raised fists over heads, Khalid was perfectly still. Alvin wished he could see the boy's face. He seemed so very young.

Alvin went to the garage and opened the long, flat wooden case where he kept his butchering tackle. He surveyed the contents: fillet knife, boning knife, a cleaver as heavy as a hatchet, a carver, a simple and gently curved butcher knife. None of these would slice through a cow's thick neck, not neatly. The cut would have to be smooth, straight, decisive. The boy's hand would have to be steady. Not one of them could handle a thrashing cow.

Then he thought of the thirty-inch blade from his riding lawn mower, and spent the rest of the afternoon sharpening it, in the backyard so as not to upset the cow. Round and round, on one side and then the other, Alvin honed the blade against the whetstone. There could be no nicks or dull spots. He knew from cutting his own hands so many times that the dull knives hurt worse, while he never felt the nick of a sharp one at all. So he sharpened and sharpened, took a break for a glass of wine, and sharpened some more.

The boy came early in the afternoon. "Mama sent this," he said. He had an armful of old newspapers and a nearly empty roll of butcher paper.

Before sending him home, Alvin took him out to the garage. With the garage light on, they both looked smaller, the boy and the cow, big but not quite fully grown. Maybe they could handle her. Maybe the boy could handle her. He had thick arms, and she really seemed to be a placid cow.

The cow pissed, loud as a rainstorm on the concrete floor, and Khalid jumped back from her. "She almost splashed me," he said. Then he said, "Gross," and the word sounded silly and even more American dressed up in the boy's lilting accent. Alvin had heard his grandchildren say it hundreds of times, about ponce, and chicken livers, and the orange-yellow fat of crawfish tails, among other things. It was a silly word, in any case.

"That's gross, yeah," Alvin said. "I'll hose it off tomorrow. Come here, boy." He handed Khalid the lawn mower blade to make him understand. "You think you can do that, what your momma wants? You think you can, boy?"

Khalid balanced the blade on his flattened palms with his fingers stretched back, away from the edge. He looked incredulously at Alvin. "You know she was joking," the boy said. "They don't do this in Sudan."

At eight in the evening, the neighborhood began to gather in Della's kitchen where she sat steadfast on a stool by the stove, stirring hot praline goo with one hand and doling out wine with the other. Claude and Pearl came first, with a loaded shotgun and the A-frame gibbet, which the men quickly installed in the garage. When Alvin saw the shotgun, he motioned for Claude to follow him to the backyard. He pointed to the long, sharp blade lying across an old sycamore stump.

"For them Indians," Claude said, "you'd do that?"

"They're from Sudan," Alvin said. "She'll call the cops if we don't let the boy do it." This was a lie, of course, and Alvin hated to tell it, but he knew that no diplomatic somersaults in French or English, no Arabic invocation of community could justify such a strange decision to Claude. Claude picked up the blade and strummed it with his thumb. "Be careful," Alvin said. "It's sharp, sharp."

"It better be sharp," Claude said.

There was a small crowd gathered in the driveway when the neighborhood policeman pulled over to the curb and rolled down his window.

"How y'all?" he called, and cracked good-natured jokes about drunken old Cajuns until his own grandmother came out of the house and pressed a bottle of homemade wine and a tin of pralines, still warm, into his hands.

"Go bring that to your wife," she said, and then, without a twitch, "Y'all still looking for them cows?"

"They still can't find some of 'em," her grandson said.

"They done got ate, I bet you."

The policeman drove away and his grandmother came back to the group, laughing from her rolling belly. "Us coonasses been stealing cows since the dawn of time," she said. "That's part of our culture, that."

Most of them laughed, but some, Claude especially, speculated in French that the brown woman had called that cop after all, that he was reconnoitering and most certainly would be back.

By nine o'clock, Alvin and Della's house was teeming, the table crowded with food. Many had brought the Saturday paper, which featured on the front page a photograph of yesterday's accident: a dead steer roped by the neck, dangling from an overpass. They would use this page, they decided with glee, to wrap up their takings this evening.

From time to time, Alvin checked on the cow. She had been quiet all day, but now with so much commotion just outside, she huffed and stomped her feet. Alvin, who could not stand to see an animal suffer, cooed at her in French and patted her flaring nose. He had not given her anything to eat or drink—she would clean easier that way—and wondered how thirsty she was, exactly. When he held a mixing-bowl full of wine under her nose, she sniffed it, tested it with

234

her tongue, then drank up every drop and flipped the bowl looking for more. Alvin gave her more.

At ten o'clock, the crowd, pressed elbow to elbow in the steamy kitchen, quieted down. The ominous booming from the students' passing cars shook the windows and pulsed in the chests of the old people like tribal drums. There had been no word from Slug or the Sudanese. Della called Slug's house but got no answer, and none of them could spell *Nasraddin* to find it in the phone book.

Had they been in their own homes, rather than here in Della's kitchen, those who lived across the street from the Nasraddins might have looked into Fatima's brightly lit living room and seen her winding bold cloths around her daughters, combing out and braiding their long hair, before she finally took up a roll of bandages and, with blunt efficiency—as though grooming her children, packing groceries, slaughtering cows, and disinfecting old men's lesions were all the selfsame gesture—ministered to the ruined face of her neighbor as he sat on her couch and hid behind his hands to spare the little girls. The spies then might have pulled shut their drapes quickly, embarrassed, when they saw Fatima glance out her own window, searching the shadows for her son, who had not returned from Mr. Guilbeau's that afternoon.

And had the people all over this neighborhood been watching from their windows, as they were accustomed to do after nightfall, flipping on their porch lights and peering out at their street, hands cupped around eyes, they would have seen a figure moving in and out of the orange light of street lamps and trespassing fearlessly into one yard after another. What a shock they'd have had when the face drew close to their windows, as close as they had ever imagined ominous faces in the night, and gazed at them; no, not at them—beyond them, into their homes, at their plain and barely valuable things. And the old couple who lived in the gray brick house on the corner—what would they have done, what would they have thought, when the expression on that face changed suddenly from curiosity to anger, when the young man at their window reared back the baseball bat he carried and swung it with a grown man's strength into the glass?

Under the light of a single bald bulb dangling from a rafter, the neighborhood gathered into Alvin's garage and formed a broad circle around the cow. They watched Alvin offer her another bowlful of wine. They watched Claude cross to the center of the circle, shotgun in hand.

It had gotten around, what the brown woman wanted. Everyone knew, and agreed to allow it. There was beef in this world, they reasoned, before there were guns; people must have killed cows somehow. As the night grew later, though, they began to believe that they had been fooled, not through spitefulness on Fatima's part, but rather through their own provincial ignorance of foreign places and customs; they hadn't gotten her joke. They had been propelled by momentum into this circle and this ritual that was at once familiar and very strange, but now as they saw Claude aiming the shotgun after all, their momentum flagged.

Claude set the shotgun aside. He said to Alvin, "Somebody will hear it. If that cop comes by, what do you want to do?"

Alvin took the lawn mower blade from where it lay on top of a deep freezer. "If you hold her head up, I'll do it. She won't feel a thing."

One of the men suggested his teenage son hold the gun aimed at the cow, just in case, and this seemed like a reasonable compromise.

Claude held her gently but firmly by the jaws. Turning the blade this way and that, switching it from hand to hand, Alvin walked around to one side of the cow, and then the other. He draped one arm over the cow's neck and poised the blade under her throat, but he could find no leverage. He stood back and considered as Claude hummed and massaged her broad buttery jowls. The teenager stood poised with the shotgun on his shoulder. They all prayed he would not shoot Claude by accident.

"Hit her in the head with something," the teenager said.

From the dark perimeter of the circle, his father said, "Hush, boy."

"I can't watch, me," Della said. She cringed back with all her body.

Alvin stood farther back. "Somebody look for that cop," he said.

Della rushed to the door and opened it just a crack. "Oh!" she squeaked.

Hearts pounded and fluttered all around the circle.

"Oh!" Della said again. "Oh, *chère*! I didn't know you at first. Come in!"

When they saw Slug, most of them for the first time in several years, the people of the neighborhood were less surprised by the bandages and deformity of Slug's face than by the young man who came in right behind him, hanging on to Slug's sagging belt.

It was Slug who had gone looking and heard the shattering glass, who had found Khalid in a dark house picking up and examining all the small, un-incriminating remnants of desk drawers and bookshelves. Somewhere in the circle now, the boy realized, was the old couple whose check stubs and prayer lists he had handled, whose refrigerator he had opened and closed, who would believe it was the work of those high school boys, drunk on a Saturday night, when they later found their window broken and things upset. Khalid let go of Slug's belt and stood up straight, seeing no one and nothing but the cow and the blade cocked under her throat.

Fatima followed, with her two little girls, all three draped in bright fabrics. A silk veil covered Fatima's head and black hair. To the neighborhood, which had seen her only in uniforms—tired, bagging groceries—Fatima seemed in these foreign clothes strangely like the Virgin Mother.

Slug's one eye winked at all of them as he looked around the circle. When his eye landed on them, they wondered, each in turn, why they had not knocked louder at his door, or longer, why no one had insisted on driving him to doctors, or cleaning his house, or helping him change his bandages.

Like an altar boy presenting the Bible, Alvin held the blade out to Khalid.

"Take it," Slug said, and Khalid picked up the blade.

Alvin lunged for a mop bucket near the door and positioned it on the ground under the cow's head. They all knew it would never contain the blood. Alvin took the shotgun from the teenager, who stepped back into the circle, pressed

238

close to his father. Alvin aimed, just in case. Claude cupped his hands around the cow's jaws again. He pulled her head up so the skin on her neck stretched flat, taut. Slug and the boy stood by her side, on the right. The boy was losing his color. He held the blade feebly. It trembled in his hands.

The neighborhood watched the boy move his lips, but no words came out.

The mother said, "Khalid—*Bismillah Ar-Rahman.*"

The boy tried again. His face blanched.

Slug laid his hand over the boy's. He hugged the boy against his chest, pressed him tightly to stop his quaking. The cow snorted. She stepped back and nearly broke free of Claude's hold. They all heard the shuffle and click when Alvin set the shotgun.

Slug and the boy cocked the blade at the cow's neck. She pounded one hoof and took a deep breath that swelled her, and as she started to moo, Slug and the boy leaned forward together.

"Y'all say a prayer," Slug said.

The blade wrenched across the tight white line of throat, like a bow on a silent fiddle. Claude stroked her cheeks while blood gushed from her neck, saturated his jeans, and pooled in the bucket at his feet. The bucket filled and spilled over, and the pool spread fast, outward and outward to Slug and the boy who had fainted in his arms, to Alvin, to Della, to Fatima and her wide-eyed girls, to the circle's perimeter, to the feet of the people who watched and remembered the country farms, the spoken French, the good of home-stuffed sausage. The blood spread out toward the garage doors, and under the doors, out to the driveway, into the street. Enough blood, they all thought, to flood the neighborhood.

These stories originally appeared, sometimes in different form, in the following publications: "Cut Off, Louisiana: A Ghost Story" in *American Short Fiction;* "The Ranger Queen of Sulphur" in *Ecotone;* "When Pluto Lost His Planetary Status" in *Gulf Coast;* "Camera Obscura" in *Nimrod;* "Poke Salad" in *Oxford American;* "The Boucherie" in *StoryQuarterly;* and "So This Is Permanence" in *Tin House.* "The Boucherie," "Camera Obscura," and "So This Is Permanence" were also reprinted in *New Stories from the South,* and "The Boucherie" was subsequently included in *Best of the South: From Ten Years of New Stories of the South.*

Acknowledgments

For the gift of time and support, without which none of these stories could have been written: the National Endowment for the Arts, the Illinois Arts Council, the St. Botolph Foundation, the Vermont Studio Center, and the Camargo Foundation. For making room for me in their pages: the editors at *Tin House, Oxford American, Nimrod International Journal, Gulf Coast, StoryQuarterly,* and *Ecotone.*

I am especially grateful to the Fine Arts Work Center in Provincetown and the Wallace Stegner Fellowship for giving me a lifelong community of smart, generous, blindingly talented writers, and to my mentors at Stanford University, Tobias Wolff and Elizabeth Tallent, whose insights always but always made these stories better.

I want to thank my sharp-eyed fellow writers, without whom this collection would be a shambles: Molly Antopol, Will Boast, Harriet Clark, Rob Ehle, Sarah Frisch, Jim Gavin, Skip Horack, Vanessa Hutchinson, Amy Keller, Abigail Ulman, Justin St. Germain, Stacey Swann, J. M. Tyree, and Jesmyn Ward.

I'm so grateful for the faith, patience, and tough love of my agent Rebecca Gradinger and for the abiding enthusiasm of my editor Ben George, who has been a champion of these stories from the beginning. Thank you, as well, to the mighty teams at Fletcher & Co. and Little, Brown, whose unflagging dedication has gotten this book out into the world at a very strange, sad, and difficult time.

For first encouraging the little glimmer of something you saw in my writing and in me: Bill Veeder, Laura Demanski, and Kenneth and Syll-Young Olson. For giving me the most important advice anyone has ever given me about writing, and for sharing your thoughts, your time, and your kindness so freely while we were lucky enough to have you on this earth: Jim McPherson.

For friendship, for readership, for bikes and hikes and canoe trips down wrong rivers, for shrimp n' grits and oyster nights, for slugging whiskey by a fire and martinis on a back porch and rosé on a Mediterranean terrace, for *meubles,* for the kind of long, winding talks that make my fiction, my world, and my spirit so much bigger and gladder: Natalie Bakopoulos, Rebecca Gayle Howell, Dana Kletter, Neal Fisher, Vance Smith, Ethan Jackson, Jorge Sánchez, Johnny Schmidt, Skye Lavin, Joe Pan, Ron Schmidt, Emily Mitchell, Laura Eve Engel, Laura McKee, Elizabeth Bradfield, Josh Rivkin, and Erin Beeghly. For being my first beloved friends, interlocutors, and co-conspirators: Lynne Kuemmel and Ellen Sung.

For raising me up, telling me stories, making me laugh, and keeping the lights of home lit up bright: Maudrie and Herman Soileau, Sandy and Ronnie Kramer, Greg and Faye Soileau, Tressa Crooks, Megan Crooks Shillow, Dyann Martin Antony and Steven Antony, Susan and Dean Wallace, Margaret and Jesse Green, Byron Nelson, and all those Simons and Fergusons and Landrys and LeBlancs in the good-hearted village on the corner of Center and East LaGrange. For giving me another home to go to: Ruth Thibodeau and Richard Gendron.

For being the women I count on in every way, every day, my chosen family, my Graces: Bergen Anderson, Laura Dixon Gallinari, Megan Levad, and Elizabeth Wetmore.

For loving my writing and for loving me: Jonah Gendron. For being a funnier, braver, smarter, more delightful kid than any I could have imagined: Adelaide Gendron. I'm a lucky, lucky lady.

About the Author

Stephanie Soileau's work has appeared in *Glimmer Train, Oxford American, Ecotone, Tin House, New Stories from the South,* and other journals and anthologies, and has been supported by fellowships from the Wallace Stegner Foundation, the National Endowment for the Arts, and the Fine Arts Work Center in Provincetown. She holds an MFA from the Iowa Writers' Workshop and has taught creative writing at the Art Institute of Chicago, Stanford University, and the University of Southern Maine. Originally from Lake Charles, Louisiana, Stephanie now lives in Chicago and teaches at the University of Chicago.